LATE IN THE SEASON

Visit us at www.boldstrokesbooks.com

LATE IN THE SEASON

by

Felice Picano

2009

LATE IN THE SEASON

ISBN 10: 1-60282-082-1
ISBN 13: 978-1-60282-082-1

THIS TRADE PAPERBACK ORIGINAL IS PUBLISHED BY
BOLD STROKES BOOKS, INC.
P.O. BOX 249
VALLEY FALLS, NY 12185

FIRST BOLD STROKES PRINTING: JUNE 2009

CREDITS
PRODUCTION DESIGN: STACIA SEAMAN
COVER DESIGN BY SHERI (GRAPHICARTIST2020@HOTMAIL.COM)

Chapter One

It was a perfect day for composing. The morning mist had finally burned off the ocean, unfurling the blue sky like a huge banner of victory. Kites were fluttering at various levels of the warm, balmy air. From down the beach came the sweet-voiced distortions of children's cries in play—the last children of the season—adding extra vibrancy to their sounds, piercing the scrim of post-Labor-Day-weekend silence that had softly dropped a week ago. Already the first dying leaves of an autumn that came early to the seashore and would blaze madly for a mere month of picture-book beauty had flung themselves at the glass doors this morning. They had saddened Jonathan then, perched over his large mug of coffee, feeling the hot sun on his closed eyelids. But now the morning felt so clear and sunny, so absolutely cloudless, he felt he might strike it with the little glass pestle in the dining room bowl, and the day would ring back, echoing crystal, like a gamelan orchestra.

Sixty fresh sheets of newly scored, oversize paper lay on the table in front of him—unstirred on the oceanside deck by any wind. Next to them was a stenographer's open flap spiral notebook, its pages filled with sketches of melodies and modulations, with samples of instrumental combinations he would incorporate into the score—jottings from the entire summer. He'd already written out many solos. Half would go into the score intact; the rest would have to be completed, revised according to the hieroglyphic notes he'd made over the past few months. Orchestral introductions and instrumental transitions would be required. But the most difficult numbers were done: the laughing quartet for male voices, Fiammetta's lament, the six madrigals the chorus would sing, commenting on the principals' actions, and furthering the flavor of thirteenth-century Florence. Barry would love them. So would Amadea and Saul, producers of *The Lady and the Falcon,* their fourth show together, the first to be written for Broadway.

Above him, to the left, there was a rippling flutter like a stricken bird's panic of feathers. A black, bat-shaped kite with two yellow eyes painted on it was falling from the highest airdraft, spinning foward, bucking, dropping through current after current. Jonathan thought it would plummet endlessly, struggling all the way down like a living thing, until it hit the sea-stained gray board roof of the Locke family's summer house next door. But the kite swept up suddenly, caught a draft, righted itself, then floated serenely on slacker line, its plastic wings unwrinkled.

Jonathan quickly wrote at the top of one score page "Gentile's Prayer," then began to fill in the tenor's vocal line, moving steadily across the page and down half a staff and only stopping at bar sixteen for the break. Last night he'd gotten away from the others in the house long enough to get down to the ocean's edge. There he'd walked, his hands shoved in his pockets, the sweatshirt flapping around his torso; there, too, he'd heard the last cries of migrating birds repeating certain phrases against the solid bass line of surf, phrases that had reminded him of a Landini arietta from seven centuries ago. Their plaintive rise and fall had unconsciously become the tenor line of Gentile's hopeless prayer.

Now he began to write in the bass continuo. That was easy until the break, so he moved up to the alto line: a high oboe that would accompany the singer over low strings. The break should lead to a more agitated central section: music like Dan last night when he came down to the water's edge and asked Jonathan to return to the house, to the others. It was their last night together for a while, Dan had reminded Jonathan almost guiltily. Yes, this central section would be anxious, sad, recalling how guilty Dan felt going away again, and his barely disguised alarm that Jonathan was taking it far too easily. That, and Dan's usual considerate fear that his life, his concerns, his career, his friends and family were taking up too much of his lover's now valuable creative time. All that Gentile would somehow express to his beloved Fiammetta on the embarkation eve of his quest for the fabled falcon.

Now for the final section—the resigned but hopeful return of the initial theme in a new key. What would that sound like?

Suddenly there was a sound like a loud slap of rubber behind him, loud enough to break his concentration. Jonathan didn't have to turn to know it was Dan, slamming open the sliding doors. No one else did it quite so forcefully.

"Jonathan, do you know where my shaving kit is?"

"Bottom left-hand drawer. You put it there when you came back from L.A. Remember?"

"I looked there."

"Under the rugby shirts. Haven't you packed them? You'll need them, you know. It'll be cooler in London."

"I'll go look again," Dan said, but his tone of voice said he'd never find the shaving kit.

"Want me to?"

"No. You're busy. I'm sorry to bother you while you're working."

Jonathan got up, weighted the score with an ashtray, and went to where Dan had just stepped inside the doorway. Dan was dressed in an open-necked shirt, casual slacks, and sports jacket. He'd be flying directly to the airport, where he'd board a jet.

"I'll look," Jonathan said. "It's no trouble." He went past Dan into the house. "When's your plane?"

"Not till one."

"It's almost noon now. Are you packed?"

"All but the shaving kit."

In their large bedroom two suitcases were open on the bed. They appeared to be neatly, fully packed, but Dan was so distracted lately, it would be just like him to forget something essential—socks, or underwear. They ought to be checked.

Jonathan rummaged through the wide bottom drawer, pushing aside various shirts, some of them wrapped in thin paper from the laundry, others still encased in plastic from their purchase. Why didn't Dan wear these shirts when they looked so good on him? Jonathan always thought his own body too stocky for them. On the bottom, shoved between two of them but bulkily apparent, was the shaving kit. Surely Dan had seen it?

"You were right," Dan said, receiving the kit, "as usual!" He stood looking at the shiny cracked leather kit in Jonathan's palms, until Jonathan thought he was going to say something: admit he'd known where it was all along and merely wanted Jonathan's company. Then Dan made a typical wry smile and hugged him, crushing the kit between them.

"Who's going to find my shaving kit for me in London?" he asked, low, against the nape of Jonathan's neck. Dan smelled of cologne today; for the trip, Jonathan supposed. Last night, after their guests had gone home, they'd put the dishes in the washer and slowly, expertly made love for hours as only couples who've been together years knew how to do. Last night Dan had smelled of almond cold cream soap, chocolate, Brie, and lust.

"You'll be all right in London."

"I always feel as though I'm missing an arm or leg or something when I'm away from you too long."

"It's only a month."

"I don't want to go," Dan said. He still held him, continued to nuzzle against his neck. The kit began to fall and Jonathan let it drop.

"You'll feel better about it when you're on the plane. You know how excited you get once you're flying."

Dan pulled back, still holding Jonathan, staring at his face. His own face was so familiar Jonathan wondered if he could ever forget it. Dan was tanned, of course—honey tan—they both were. His left eyebrow had two long bright orange hairs sticking out of the surrounding chestnut like little signal flags. Dan's long nose and forehead were slightly freckled, even through his tan; his forelock and mustache tinged with vague touches of gray that almost seemed blond. All the rest was the same face that Jonathan had looked at for almost a decade: the country boy urbanized, sophisticated, grown up.

"What are you thinking?" Dan asked.

"How good-looking you are."

"Still am, you mean?"

"Yes."

"Do you think we'll always look twenty-seven years old to each other?" Dan asked.

Jonathan wanted to say no, that Dan no longer looked twenty-seven, that he looked his age: thirty-five. Dan had grown older and Jonathan liked that. Dan's self-assured smirk had mellowed into a wry mature grin; his bright arrogant look was only occasionally present, replaced by a trusting, comfortable gaze.

"I suppose," Jonathan said. "Go pack the shaving kit before you forget."

"Aren't we going to have a big parting scene?"

"Here? I thought we'd save that for the seaplane dock."

"You're coming? I thought you'd be busy composing."

"I'll come."

"You don't have to."

"I'll come," Jonathan said. "I'll weep and wave a tearstained handkerchief as the seaplane flies off into the sunset. It will be very touching, terribly domestic."

Dan stared, then laughed.

"You're nuts." A quick hug, then he picked up the shaving kit and went to the bathroom to fill it with toiletries.

So, he had known where it was all the while. He'd thought that Jonathan would let him go away without saying a private good-bye.

Jonathan checked through the packed bags anyway, hearing Dan happily whistling in the bathroom.

"Don't forget the allergy pills," Jonathan called out. The bags were well packed: there was even a pocket-size chessboard. Evidently Dan wasn't taking chances on boring flight companions. Jonathan zipped the bags, brought them outside, plumped them into the little red-and-white Radio Flyer wagon, then went around to the front deck, gathered up all his papers, and carried them inside.

"It's getting late," he called, then went out again. The day was beginning to cool. It seemed slightly gray in the west, where he could sometimes see weather approaching them a week in advance.

"How about a drink for the road?" Dan asked. He had his flight bag slung over his shoulder and held a bottle of vodka.

"Don't you take Valiums for the plane?"

"Oh, all right." Dan came out onto the deck without the bottle. He threw his free arm around Jonathan's shoulder. "When I come back you'll have the whole score done, won't you?"

"I hope."

"I do too. I was thinking last night how this would be a good thing, my going off like this alone for a month. I'll be busy. You'll be busy. You know how much I hate to see the summer end. I'll come back to glorious autumn. You'll be done. We can be together again, and I won't have to apologize all the time."

Dan kept talking as they pulled the wagon along the wooden plank boardwalks that encircled and formed the only paths in their autoless community. Jonathan kept his free arm around Dan's waist, his fingers hooked into Dan's belt loop, as they descended the incline, leveled off, passed houses he saw every day, telephone poles, trees he'd remembered blooming wildly earlier in the summer.

Everything Dan said made sense. He understood that Jonathan now needed privacy and solitude to do his work; that when he returned the pressure would be off, and they would be able to deal with each other again completely, without the score between them all the time. Look at me, Jonathan wanted to say to the few people they passed, look at me and my handsome, mature lover, who understands me better than I do myself at times.

The seaplane was already at the dock. Someone took the bags off the wagon and placed them in the rear compartment of the big metal and fiberglass craft. Dan dropped his bag onto the seat, then stood on the pier. Two passengers were already belted in. The pilot was talking to a local woman. The dock was otherwise empty.

"Now if I don't come back," Dan began, "you know where the

will is. I keep the safety deposit box keys at the bottom of the safe. All my papers are in order. My family won't give you any trouble. They're provided for."

"And I'll have you cremated and scatter your ashes on Forty-second Street."

"I could *die,* you know," Dan said, suddenly offended.

"And I could get married and sire three bouncing babies."

"In a month?"

"Well, I could make a start."

"Would you name a boy for me?"

"Sure. Dan Two. Or better, Dead Dan the Second."

"I once dreamed you died," Dan said. "Remember when you were in the hospital? I dreamed they gave you the wrong stuff, instead of anesthetic, and when I came to visit you the next morning they had a sheet over you. I felt so awful. Sort of like being in a really bad Lana Turner movie, where she mopes and wears lots of black chiffon. Then I tried to picture my life without you. And you know what? I couldn't. I'd open a kitchen cabinet looking for paper towels, and you'd be there, winking at me. I'd open a closet for a pair of pants, and you'd be standing there, shaking your head at my choice."

"Stop," Jonathan said.

"Even in the dream I couldn't begin to think of what I'd do without you."

"Stop! You're not going to die in a plane crash, and I'm not going to die either. At least not for a while. Go to London."

He kissed Dan.

"Go to London. Get rich and famous."

The pilot got in, then Dan. Jonathan unhooked the dock line and the seaplane turned with the tide and floated parallel to the dock, out into the mainstream of the bay, very slowly. Dan looked out his window, but didn't wave, as the pilot revved up the motor. The plane began to slide forward, its pontoons skimming the sun-shattered water. Then it began to lift slightly, tilting from side to side a bit, and finally it rose, leveled off, swerved slightly, and flew over the bay.

Jonathan remained on the dock until the seaplane was a speck against the darkening sky. Then he walked back to his house. Turning into his yard, he noticed the neighbors' deckchairs were out. He'd thought the Lockes were gone for the season. Hadn't they closed up the house last week? Maybe not.

It was too hot to work on the deck, so he made himself a vodka tonic, and sipped it slowly, listening to some medieval music on the cassette deck. Then it began to cloud over, and he felt exhausted. The bedroom seemed suddenly abandoned without Dan's carelessly thrown clothing everywhere. Jonathan felt very at sea for a minute.

"I'm a lucky man to have a lover like Dan," he said to himself. Then he fell asleep.

CHAPTER TWO

It was a mistake to come out here, Stevie thought, as soon as she stepped out of the ferry onto the landing dock.

Only five or six passengers had come across the bay with her, sparsely settling the big upstairs deck, making it seem even emptier. On the Sea Mist side, no one was waiting—no greeting families, no welcoming husbands, wives, lovers, boyfriends. Only a large sheepdog with a bandanna tied around its shaggy neck was sitting on its haunches, as though expecting its master. It stood up to sniff the legs of the departing passengers, then settled back to continue waiting.

Despite the few people, it was still pleasant being here, Stevie said to herself, determined to go through with what she'd begun. She only had a light weekend shoulder bag to carry, so she didn't bother unlocking or unchaining her family's wagon from its dockside hitching post at the harbor. And the walk to her family's house, though solitary, was fine. The leaves were beginning to turn here already; the poison ivy was a blood red. The air was fresh. A large bird—a magpie?—was sitting on a high wire, chattering at her. She whistled a bit at it until it cocked its head, gave a short squawk, and flew off. Had she meant to send it off?

"You don't know your own mind, Stevie." The words came back to her, her mother's words, last night; then again, this morning, in the big breakfast room, four stories above Gramercy Park.

"I do too!" Stevie had replied, fiercely. She said it again now, walking along the boardwalk, hitching the shoulder strap of her bag higher. "I do too!"

"You'll regret your decision," her father had said, shaking his head morosely over his French toast. "Believe me, Stevie."

And so she replayed the whole argument. Last night's with her parents, then later on, on the phone with Bill—God! that horrible conversation! He'd sounded as though she'd shoved a knitting needle into his heart—then again with her parents this morning.

She turned off the main walkway and onto the one leading toward the ocean, to her family's summer house. Old furniture, a battered refrigerator, torn and buckled plastic lounge chairs, old wood sheets from a torn-down partition, all lay in a heap at the corner, strewn there for the heavy garbage pickup. She wondered if they'd left any firewood in the house when they closed up. Just like them not to. Boy, her parents were thorough. They never missed a touch, did they? They'd manipulated and cajoled and controlled Liz and Jerry's lives already, beyond hope, Stevie thought. Now they'd started on her.

"You're only eighteen," her mother had sighed. "You don't have to know your own mind. But listen to me, or at least to your father. We know better."

Sure. They knew better. They knew what they wanted, that was all. They'd wanted Jerry to be a doctor, and now he was interning at Lenox Hill Hospital. They'd wanted Liz married to Tony Halle, and she was. They'd wanted Stevie at Smith College this afternoon to begin her sophomore year—another year! then two more!—and then they wanted her to marry Bill Tierney.

The bushes in the path off the walk to her family's house had grown out. She had to brush past them to get by. Funny how fast they grew so late in the summer. Her father—her meticulous father—would have pruned them the last time he was here—Labor Day weekend.

Ah! and here it was: the house! Her house now. All to herself.

Her spirits rose seeing the darling, old, irregular gray clapboard house. She'd always loved it as a child, had missed not being here at all this summer, having to spend time weekends with Bill and his family at their house in the Thimble Islands in Connecticut. Or with Liz and her kids in Syosset. Now Stevie walked three-quarters around the house, looking into every curtained window as though she were a stranger, someone coming to buy it, or to inspect it, or rob it. Before going in, she climbed the ladder to the roofdeck—really a sort of widow's walk—her father and brother and Bill had added on in front a few years ago. This was her favorite spot; she had come up here a great many times, trying to get away from the others, to sit undisturbed watching the ocean.

She would come up here again, later, at sunset, with a cup of hot tea, and watch the geese migrating south, across a parti-colored island sky.

From her perch, she heard a humming, and turned to see a white seaplane rise up over the treetops like a tiny bright dragonfly before it turned slightly, and smoothly glided toward the city.

How peaceful it was. The ocean seemed almost calm: majestic, perfectly ordinary, yet always wonderful. All the foliage had grown so much this year, the nearest houses seemed like enchanted cottages hidden away in spellbound forests that required secret passwords to penetrate.

The Galgianos' house had never looked so still. The windswept decks looked bleak without their colorful chairs and bathing cushions and bikini-clad occupants. Farther away, two small partly attached houses belonging to the Winstons were closed. The entire stretch of beach in front of her perch was empty. She'd walk there later. She loved walking along empty beaches. How long had it been since she'd done it—been allowed to do it—alone? Two years? It seemed so long ago.

Only the lovers' house seemed open: unshuttered, uncurtained, furniture still placed out on the decks: the big, handsome lounges from Hammacher Schlemmer, the large mahogany table, the elegant smaller tables, the slant board and weights neatly spaced to one side. She called them the lovers, but they had names, of course: Jonathan Lash and Daniel Halpirn. Sometimes she called Daniel David by mistake, thinking of the Biblical lovers, and all three of them would register the error and be pleased, and laugh. She called them the lovers to her parents, to her friends, to Bill, and in front of his family. Openly, declaratively, defiantly, at times. In such a way that none of their euphemisms could get by. Not "those nice men," or "that couple," but the lovers; as if she were in on a secret conspiracy with Jonathan and Daniel to keep what they really were as clear, as obvious as possible.

Leave it to the lovers to still be here after Labor Day. They knew what was good, what was truly valuable. Not the noisy, crowded Sunday August afternoons when everyone within a hundred-mile radius would arrive on the beach. But now, still hot and clear, even lovelier, in mid-September.

Well, at least she'd have their company in this isolation. Not of course that she'd visit them or anything like that. She hadn't much in summers past, and only with Bill and Jerry for the big party the lovers had thrown last year. No, she'd see them, though: on the walkways, on the beach perhaps, on their deck having dinner or reading, or lifting weights. That would be enough for her—just a wave. Hi! Hi Lovers! Hi Jonathan! Hi Daniel!

She was here to be alone.

"You're going out there alone?" Bill had asked last night. "It'll be desolate!"

"That's just what I want, Bill, to be alone," she'd replied. "To be away from you and my parents. To get away from all the pressures."

"Do what you want," he answered, his voice turning that into a challenge, a threat. "Do whatever you want. You'll be bored after one day out there."

She hated Bill for that remark.

Her mother had been a bit better about it. That morning, when Stevie had asked for the keys to the summer cottage, her father had stared at her, perplexed. Her mother had turned out of the breakfast room and come back with the keys, and had given them to Stevie without a word. She hadn't said a word after, when Stevie went to her bedroom, packed, or when she waved good-bye and went downstairs to grab a taxi to Penn Station for the train out here.

Naturally her mother thought she'd go crazy out here alone too.

But at least she thought her way was better: giving Stevie the rope to hang herself.

"What is it precisely that you want?" Bill had asked.

"I don't know. But I know what I don't want," Stevie had answered firmly.

"Me? You don't want me?" he'd asked.

She'd sighed then: he was so dense. "Oh, I don't know, Bill. I just don't want to be railroaded. That's all."

"Railroaded?"

"Railroaded into college, into marriage, into friends that I've had all my life. I want to explore a little. I will not end up like my sister Liz."

He hadn't understood, naturally. He'd thought she didn't love him.

Did she?

"Let's not get into that yet," Stevie said out loud. "We have time to figure that out. Plenty of time."

How could anyone not like Bill Tierney? He was bright, ambitious, capable, funny, at times charming, attractive, presentable on most occasions. Above all, he was in love with her. Yet...Yet... He'd arrived so early in her life. Too early. She'd dreamed of long courtships with a variety of men in various locales before she would settle down. Affairs with hippies in Munich and Amsterdam; with ranchhands in Montana with faces cracked like old leather; with established, older men, powerful financiers or leaders in the arts, on Caribbean islands. Not this instant, total romance at seventeen with a boy—yes, a boy!—three years older whom everyone agreed was a perfect match for her.

It was beginning to cloud up. Getting cool too. It still might not spoil the glorious sunset she longed to see; but she'd better do that beach walk now.

The key turned easily. Inside, the house wasn't even musty, as it was at the beginning of the season: only a little damp and closed smelling.

She opened windows, brought her bag into her bedroom, dropped it on the bed, and began checking for clothing left out here.

A blue short-sleeve sweatshirt lay in one drawer. An old nylon blue racing bikini, wrapped in a towel in another. A bright orange slicker hung in her closet. Nothing else.

They would all be gathering at the dorms tonight: Jennie, Alice, Beth, Maria. They'd be in and out of each other's rooms, sitting on beds, gossiping about their summers as they unpacked and hung up their clothing, showing off new purchases to each other, already deciding on trade-offs. They'd all be wondering where she was—why she was so late this semester—their bright, naughty, sophisticated New York City pal, Stevie Locke.

God! How horrible memories were, Stevie thought. How really horrible it will be when I'm eighty-five, with all those memories crowding around me. No wonder Grandma Locke walks around as though in a daze most of the time. All those memories to bump against, to shake off, to evade, to steer through.

She had work to do out here, she recalled. Important, crucial work. Decisions to be made about Bill, about Smith College, about going to work, about leaving home. She would take a week to decide. No longer. But she would decide. Then act on those decisions.

Fortified by her resolution, she went into the kitchen, brewed a pot of tea, went through the kitchen cabinets checking for food. She found crackers and jelly, discovered a paperback mystery on the living room game shelf, and settled in for the afternoon, reading and eating. Once she looked up to check the fireplace. Meticulous Daddy had left half a compressed log.

She'd get more tomorrow. Go shopping for food too. For now, all she could think of was that the telephone was shut off, there was no one to bother her, the ocean was regularly shuffling, and the book in her hand was totally engrossing.

Chapter Three

L ove you," Jonathan said into the humming distance of the telephone. "Bye."

He heard a crackling—a storm over the Atlantic, he supposed—then Dan's voice, distantly:

"Ta!"

"Ta!" Jonathan repeated and hung up.

Just like Daniel to already be saying "Ta!" as though he'd grown up in Holborn. He must be enjoying London. But of course he would. For some Americans, it would be all business—meetings, conferences, misunderstandings, and agreements finally reached; for others it would be all tourism. Not for Daniel. For Dan it would be glamour, respect, honor, work, admiration, command, money. Few enough American directors were invited over to do British television for Dan's trip to be special. His series on the American presidency was already being hailed, and only a quarter of the programs' scripts were even ready, never mind not a foot of film shot yet. It was to be an Anglo-American production, lasting a year, raising its director, producers, and starring actors to new eminence. It had been Daniel's brilliant idea to do the first four programs with British casts. "You know, Jonathan, the founding fathers were more Anglo than the current queen. Why, it wasn't until Andrew Jackson, really, that they even began to sound American." Good for Dan. He deserved all this attention. He'd been wasted on television films for years, used for police mystery series, assigned remakes of feature films, exploited for his ease, taste, and great love of work. Now, finally, he was going to show them how good he really was.

The Locke girl was out on the beach again. Alone again. Where were the others? Where was her boyfriend? What was his name? Bill something. He might be her fiancé by now. Hadn't her mother said something about them being engaged? That would be just like Mrs. Locke. Call me Paula, and I'll call you Jonathan. Such informality. And for what? For one afternoon together every summer, on the Lockes' most enclosed terrace deck, "saying hello again," as she put it. Those dreadful afternoons. This June, unable to face it, Daniel had taken half a Quaalude, and told Mrs. Locke through his half sleep that he was allergic to something or other and was under antihistamine sedation. Jonathan had been stuck with getting Daniel there, propping him up, translating his slurred speech, and helping carry him home again. The woman had suspected nothing. But then why would she? Her banality was all-encompassing. Yet she was a good woman, behind all that façade. Even Dan could see that, despite his name—Lady Bracknell—for her. How he'd fumed after that incident with the Locke boy, Jerry, three summers back. "She's a monster, Jonathan!" he'd ranted. "She wears two sets of balls around her neck like a Tagalog witch doctor!" Three sets now, with the boyfriend added in.

What would Paula Locke be like onstage? he wondered. Big, chesty, she'd probably sing in a low contralto, make a good character part. Like Giustina, the serving wench in *Lady and the Falcon,* a real foil for Fiammetta with her earthy humor and love of ribaldry. Yet Giustina had her soft side too. Had Jonathan shown that clearly enough? Had he characterized her musically fully enough? She had two big songs—the scolding one in the first act, and the duet with Gentile in act two. Perhaps that second solo ought to be a serenata, even a barcarolle. The gentle rocking of a boat in a wind-ruffled lagoon. A lullaby. What would Barry think of that? Jonathan would try to persuade him that it would more fully develop the character. Barry might say yes right off. Then again, he might get quiet and explanatory, which meant that when he'd written the words he'd been thinking of anything but a lullaby. Still…

The Locke girl had stood up again. This time to go into the water. Pretty bathing suit, that floral print two-piece. A languid walk to the surf. One toe poked in. A step back. A look around. Then one entire foot in the water. Reaction: another fast step back onto the sand. Another look around. Then a dash, a mad run, all arms and legs, scampering into the waves. God, it's cold for September, she must think as she dives in and under a breaker. Then up, gasping for air, another wave about to break, she holds her breath, drops straight down under it and up again, shaking her head. A smile with her realization that it really isn't that cold. Then a leisurely swim, diving, cavorting, rolling over. Christ, she was so young!

And the look on her boyfriend's face that night last summer when Daniel had dragged Jonathan off the deck and inside the house, whispering through his light martini haze, "Fuck these people; let's go neck!" In the kitchen Dan had kissed Jonathan, opened his Hawaiian shirt, and pulled his slacks half off his hips. Dan was on his knees tonguing Jonathan's navel when the boyfriend stepped in too, with empty glass and wine bottle in his hands. Even in the dim light he saw enough to make him stop still. Jonathan saw him, of course, not Dan right off. And the boyfriend's eyes were fixed so instantly, so totally on Dan's tongue, he didn't even see that Jonathan was watching him. He probably never dreamed they actually made love flesh to flesh, did he? Then Dan finally looked up and caught Jonathan's eye signal. Dan got up nonchalantly, went over to Bill, took the empty bottle, saying, "Why don't you take over for a minute, while I freshen up the vino." Jonathan thought for a moment Bill actually would, he seemed so hypnotized by then. How Dan laughed about it in bed later on. Laughed about it the rest of the summer. What would he have done, Jonathan wondered, if the boyfriend had taken over? Probably nothing. Probably made his face-slapping gesture in disapproval, and stalked out to the rest of the party, where in the midst of serving someone—Mr. Locke, perhaps—Dan would casually mention that his daughter's boyfriend had finally come to his senses and was going down on someone in the kitchen. No. He'd tell Jerry, that's who he'd tell.

Jerry Locke was a lost cause from the beginning. Jonathan

could see that. The boy was irredeemably straight from the cradle on; certainly from the day he arrived here at Sea Mist, aged fourteen or so. Three years back, the summer Dan "discovered" Jerry, as he said it, the boy was sleeping with a half-dozen women here: Miranda, the cop's wife; Mrs. McGrath; the two clerks at the boutique; Jill, who brought over the newspapers and sold them mornings at the harbor; how many more beach widows? They wouldn't let him deliver a grocery carton without at least a fast hand job. Poor kid was worn out all the time. But who could blame them? Or Dan? Jerry Locke at nineteen was at his peak. A young god. Hair blonder than a Clairol ad. So ripe, so firm, his flesh almost demanded to be stroked.

Come to think of it, all of Dan's infatuations seemed to be unobtainable, one way or another. Little Raphael, the "Frog," Jonathan called him. He hung around a few weeks, then just hopped off down the beach to another house. Sandy Wilks, the surfer. He was blond and beautiful, although something of a simpleton. Jerry Locke, of course. Perhaps if they were obtainable, truly available, Dan would have gone off with one of them. Instead, he would always turn back to Jonathan, feel comforted by his disdain of what Dan claimed to be a broken heart. Dan seemed to take real pleasure in Jonathan's refusal to acknowledge his silly affairs, his refusal to even discuss them until long afterward, and then only with total objectivity.

Ah! She was coming out of the water now, pausing in the surf to let the hot afternoon sun dry her off. The mist of the evaporation glittered on her like the ocean. Venus Aphrodite, risen from the sea. Even her position was like the Botticelli: the long fair hair swung out, one hand up to her breast, her hips slung down, one foot pointed in front. Lovely. No wonder ancient men thought some women were goddesses.

She looked up now and, spotting Jonathan on the front deck, shaded her eyes to make sure, peered, then seemed to recognize him. A shy wave, then a more positive one. Jonathan stood up and waved back. The wind off the surf furled his words of greeting to her: a simple "Hi!" from her twisted back to him like a ribbon of sound. She said something else, pointing. Dan? Was she asking after him?

Jonathan shook his head no; Dan's not here. She tilted her head. Didn't understand. Waved again, a little more hesitantly. Smiled. Then strolled to her beach blanket and slowly lay down. Lovely.

Something lovely, shy, pointed, feminine. That's what Giustina would sing. To hell with what Barry thought. It would be a barcarolle.

CHAPTER FOUR

Halfway home from the grocery store—a longish walk—Stevie began to feel raindrops. She didn't mind. It wasn't a cold rain; rather refreshingly warm, in fact. She was only wearing shorts and a halter top. She could wring them out when she got home.

It was pleasant being in the rain out here, seeing all the birds suddenly emerge from bushes and thickets and dive like small airplanes for denser cover. They would hide there, all bunched up, their heads sunk into their ruffled-up chest feathers. How nice it was in the rain out here! In the city it would be a mess: cars splashing, puddles forming at street corners, slippery subway gratings to tread cautiously over. How nice to walk barefoot over the warm wet boardwalks.

By the time she arrived back at her family's house, the raindrops had become a shower, and she was soaked. The grocery bag she carried was so wet she had to hold it underneath with both hands to keep the compressed log, carton of milk, fruits and vegetables from spilling out through water-made rips.

She changed into dry clothing. Noting that it was now somewhat cooler, she closed the windows and doors and sat in her father's big wickerwork rocking chair, watching the show of rain sheeting down onto the surf, until she was lulled to sleep.

She awoke to darkness. The rain hadn't stopped. If anything, it seemed to be raining much harder now. It rattled on the shingled roof like horses' hooves; it twisted down in great vertical sheets on the front and side decks, beating down the bushes and swirling around the cottage's corners to slap at the windows like boys with BB guns.

She'd been cold when she awakened. She put on two or three lamps, then went to the kitchen to brew a cup of warming tea. Waiting for the water to boil, she turned on the little electric clock radio and dialed through fields of static until she arrived at a voice. It was the nine o'clock news. That late?

She sat down with the tea and the mystery novel, only hearing fragments of the announcer's words, until he began reporting the weather. Heavy rain was predicted throughout the night: six inches or more. Flooding was expected in low-lying areas. Gale force winds. Small craft warnings had been posted by the Coast Guard. Odd, after such a sunny, warm, clear day, she thought.

She went to the window to look out again. The rain was coming down so hard it sheeted over the window, making it opaque. She opened it—an inch, no more—and tried to look outside. It was quite dark: she couldn't see any lights from houses in this direction. She closed it and did the same on the other side of the house. This side was more densely populated: there were a few more lights—but quite distant. The lovers, of course, were in. God! It was awful out there!

She prepared herself a light dinner, read, listened to the radio even though she didn't care for the "easy listening" stuff on this station and would have preferred rock or even jazz. It was the only one she could get without great distortion: and it *was* contact, of a sort. She would read her book, perhaps build a fire with the log she'd bought today, perhaps play solitaire, be alone, as she'd been all day. She would prove to herself, as well as to her parents and to Bill Tierney, that she could be, had to be, left alone.

Imagine Liz with those kids surrounding her all day. Tony at night. When was Liz ever alone? When the kids were at nursery school and the baby taking a midafternoon nap? For an hour, maybe less than that? Not enough time even to catch her breath.

Do I want that? Do I? Because that's what will happen to me if I marry Bill. He'll argue that's not true. He'll say we'll take it easy: not have children for a while. He'll say that I'll be able to finish school. We'll each pursue our own careers. Then, maybe after several years, we'll have children. Sure, that's what he'll say. The truth will be different. More like Liz's life.

I don't have a career, anyway. That's one problem. What's going to happen when I graduate from school? I should have listened to Uncle Ned when he suggested I go to engineering school. At least I'd be prepared for something. I don't really want to teach, which is what's expected. I don't want to—to what? To work? Maybe I don't. Or worse, maybe I don't want to grow up, period. Maybe that's what all this is about.

The radio station began to drift, and Stevie became aware of how much harder it was raining now than an hour ago when she'd awakened. She tried to retrieve the radio channel, but it was a cheap little receiver, and what she was able to hold on to was so shrill and crackling, that after a minute she had to turn it off. With the little bit of radio-induced comfort gone, she could hear the rain more clearly. It would slam down on the roof with so much force she wondered if she could hear herself speak out loud. Worse, the windows all around her would thump every once in a while as gusts of wind struck them. She moved around shutting curtains, then went back to sit in the rocker.

She felt chilly. She got up and found the sweatshirt she'd left behind, but that had short sleeves, and her arms had goose bumps. She found her work shirt and put that on underneath the sweatshirt.

"Oh, boy!" she said to her reflection in the mirror. "Don't I look stylish! Very hillbilly." She'd already gotten nice color today.

There was a distant boom, then a sheet of lightning tore across the bedroom window, brightening it. Involuntarily she jumped, then cursed her silliness in the mirror and laughed.

What a great day it had been. Alone almost all day, and not needing, not wanting any company. On the beach, the closest people had been so far away that she could barely make them out. They'd left earlier than she too. When she strolled down the beach, they'd gone, leaving a big red and white beach umbrella stuck in the sand, shading a little white metal table and two white chairs, each seating a huge stuffed animal, perched precariously on the edge of the table, as though slightly drunk and conversing. That was funny. And watching the sandpipers dipping back and forth, scampering along the water's edge always pleased her. Of course they were digging for food—some type of tiny fish or insect or even algae, she knew, with their long pointed bills. But how officious and bureaucratic they seemed: how intent too, as though they were government officials of the seashore, busily checking the sand for hardness, or strength, or granular distribution. They'd reminded her of filing clerks, secretaries, and of the one time she'd been in the vast secretarial pool at LD&G, where Bill worked. Bill was sometimes like these sandpipers. He'd peck at his food, peck at his newspaper, even peck at her body, taking little sips, checking out various spots, when they made love.

Stop! She was being terrible. She was making herself laugh at Bill's expense. It was a terrible comparison. An invidious comparison, Rose Heywood would say. Would Rose wonder where Stevie was this semester? Of course she would. Rose Heywood was the one thing to look forward to at school, really. Their little teas tête-à-tête, their occasional shopping forays to Springfield, their car rides down to New York City for the weekend, where Rose would go to clubs and cabarets and restaurants Stevie only read about in magazines.

What a wonderful teacher, what a wonderful woman Rose Heywood was! How well they liked each other, and how well they got along together, even though Rose was twelve years older and knew scads more. "Never lie about your age, dear," Rose had once said. "If you look young for it, you'll always feel complimented rather than flattered. If you look older…well, you'll always be honored for your endurance." Rose. She would see Rose anyway, wouldn't she? Even if she didn't return to Smith? But it wouldn't be the same, would it, as those mad car rides down, with Rose smoking furiously in the middle of a weekend traffic jam on the Henry Hudson Parkway? Or Rose's awful thumbnail sketches of the men sitting in the cars around them. "That one's a fetishist, Stevie. You can tell by the glazed expression in his eyes. Right now he's probably fondling himself and thinking about his secretary's instep." Or, "Secret agent if I ever saw one. Don't be fooled by the Huck Finn innocent looks. The government always goes for the boyish ones. They think they look more trustworthy. He'd as soon shoot your head off as offer you a light." Oh, Rose! Now there was an independent woman.

But did Stevie want to be like Rose? Not completely. Above all she didn't want to be totally cynical, utterly world weary as Rose sometimes seemed.

The kitchen lights suddenly flickered. When she went into the living room, the lights there flickered on and off too. She immediately began to feel afraid, then admonished herself and went to check the hurricane lamps. The one above the kitchen sink had a hairline crack in its bowl. It wouldn't work. The older one in the living room had a tiny wick, but there didn't seem to be a great deal of oil in the bowl. She lighted it just to make certain it would go on, then blew it out, turned off the oil spigot, and left the matches nearby—just in case.

The rain seemed just as bad as before, only now it had begun to thunder: not a hollow distant thunder, but short, loud cracks like the sound of huge trees splitting at their thickest part and falling. Lightning began to illuminate the room, first at one window, then at another. Stevie saw that the lightning was striking very close, into a stand of pine trees not a dozen feet from the house. She remembered her girl scout counting method for determining how close the storm center really was. Watch the lightning, then count slowly until you heard the thunder—each interval represented a mile. Another sheet of lightning tore down in the side yard, and she counted. Thunder boomed even before she reached one.

She tried tuning the radio again; it whistled so badly she had to turn it off.

She tried reading her mystery novel, but found that she couldn't concentrate.

It was foolish to feel afraid. It was just a storm. In the city, she would hardly notice it. Because there was less traffic noise here, less protection, she heard it, felt more exposed to it, that was all. It was nothing to be afraid of. And what if the electricity did finally go out. They'd had brownouts and blackouts at the summer house for years.

None had lasted more than a few hours. The hurricane lamp would last that long.

But when the lights did begin flickering again, as she was cleaning the dinner dishes, then finally flickered off, she felt afraid. She brought her just-made cup of tea out to the living room, where she lighted the lamp, opened the curtains, and even the door for a second to make sure all the other houses had suffered the same fate.

Only a dull yellow glow—from the lovers' house—consoled her for being stranded on a promontory in the middle of a terrific hurricane in the middle of the Atlantic Ocean.

The oil lamp didn't provide enough light to read by without straining her eyes. It guttered too. She attempted laying out the deck of cards for a game of solitaire, but they only reminded her of how alone she really was. Sleep would be a real escape, but could she get to sleep with all this racket, and after having had a nap?

"Serve her right," her father would be saying to her mother right now in their well-lighted apartment overlooking Gramercy Park. Her mother wouldn't protest. Stevie knew how tightly organized his system of instant retribution and justice were. How Paleolithic, really, when she thought of it. Bill Tierney was a bit like that too, sometimes. Not as rigid yet...but the potential was certainly there.

They would expect her to return to the city tomorrow, frightened, chastened, ready to go back to school, to get married, to become another zombie like Liz, just because of a storm.

The lightning seemed all around the house now. The bushes outside the window were being blown so forcefully their branches tapped the panes, like fingers striking it. She was certain she heard footsteps in the kitchen. The hurricane lamp only brightened a tiny space, hardly anything at all. Who knew what was lurking in the corners of the rooms?

There was a creak in a floorboard to her right, and Stevie froze instantly. She only relaxed after a few minutes, when it didn't repeat.

Of course it was possible for someone to have gotten in. She hadn't locked the doors until she awakened from her nap. One of those men she'd seen unloading the flatboats in the harbor. The way that tall blond bearded one had looked at her this afternoon, blankly, stupidly, as though he hated her. He might have followed her back here, come in quietly, be waiting for her in the corridor.

"No!" she gasped, standing up.

There was no response, except a sudden crack of lightning in front and the unremitting rain pounding the roof. That was even more unnerving.

I have to get out of here, she thought. Get out before I really frighten myself with all these fears and fancies. I'd be mortified if someone arrived here in a day or so to find me catatonic, hunched at the back of a clothes closet.

She carried the lamp in front of her, inspecting every room, every closet of the house, until she was satisfied she was alone. When she returned to the living room, she looked out the window, at the rain. Aside from the glow in the lovers' house, it seemed as dark as on the last day of time.

I can't, she thought. I can't. That would mean giving up, admitting I'm afraid. I won't.

A terrific burst of lightning brightened the room as though it were daylight, and at the same time thunder surrounded the house in rumbling cannonades. The lamp began to gutter.

I'll admit it. I'm terrified.

She grabbed her slicker from the closet, barely got it on and fastened before she turned off the lamp and opened the front door. Even with the hood up, she had to bend down to the latch in order to see the keyhole to lock the door.

It was awful out. She was completely out of her mind to come out here when she had a safe dry house. And the wind! She could barely keep herself from being blown off the deck.

She bent low, and tried running. The rain splashed in her face as though someone had trained a hose on her. At the entrance to the lovers' house walk, she hesitated, holding on to their deck railing to keep herself from being blown against the walls. What if they were doing something private? Making love, or something like that? Surely they didn't expect a neighborly visit in this weather.

Another crack of lightning surrounded her house in a malignant glow, making it look so eerie and repulsive that she decided. She ran along the deck, crossed her fingers, tried to wipe the rain out of her eyes enough to peer in, and gritting her teeth, knocked hard on the glass door.

CHAPTER FIVE

In the first startling moment that Jonathan realized that the new sound amid all the other racket was actually someone knocking on the glass doors, he was certain a boat had been shipwrecked. His next impression, as he got up out of his chair, pulled aside the heavy curtains, and indeed made out a gesturing, drenched, oddly attired figure, was that his first thought had been astonishingly correct.

When he unlocked and slid open the door, gusts of wind blew rain and the figure into the foyer. He made out a small man, a teenage boy, in an orange slicker. Jonathan shut the door behind the boy, and turned to see the raincoat open, the hood thrown back, the oddly familiar face—Jerry? Jerry Locke? Visiting now? Then he saw it wasn't Jerry at all; it was the Locke girl, staring helplessly at him, then at the floor where she was forming a widening puddle of water, then at her soaked denims, and finally back up at his face. For a moment he thought she was going to laugh hysterically, and he would have, in addition to the nerve-wracking noise of the rain on the roof, the howling wind, the thunder and lightning, her maniacal laughter to put up with too.

He must have looked as surprised as he actually was. He tried to settle his face into composure to meet hers. What could be the emergency that had driven her out in this weather? Was someone ill? Injured?

"Yes?" he said, drawing out the word, the question.

A torrent of words escaped from her, so fast, so confused, so incomprehensible, that he was relieved when she stopped in mid-phrase and began to cry.

He went to her, pulling off the raincoat and dropping it to the floorboards, and took the sobbing, trembling creature into the broad warmth of his cashmere-covered arms. She felt impossibly small there, fragile, like a child.

She stopped crying as quickly as she'd begun, and peeked up at him.

"It's all right. It's over," she said, sniffling, and even trying to laugh. She remained in his hug, however, until he finally felt self-conscious and let down his arms so she could stand free. "You must think I'm nuts," she said.

"I don't know…I don't know what to think yet," he admitted. "Is anything wrong?"

"Not now," she said, looking around her. She spotted the raincoat on the floor and reached for it. "Where can I hang this?" she said, holding it by an edge. "And where's the mop? I'll clean up this mess I made."

"I'll do it," he said, but didn't move.

"I was alone," she explained. The tears in her eyes had dried up. They shone clear, rather tin-colored in the candlelight. "First the radio went off," she said. "There's no phone; it was shut off Labor Day. Then the storm got worse. Then the lightning began. Then the lights went out. I was scared," she concluded.

"Ah!" he said, suddenly understanding what she was doing there—though he didn't really understand at all. Scared of what? he wanted to ask: this hurl and burl of the elements that had kept him irritated all night long, unable to concentrate on his work, unable to read, or listen to music on the cassette deck. "You were alone?"

"I guess I needed company," she said brightly, then felt embarrassed, and began to blush.

"Your jeans are all wet," he said. She was soaked from her knees down.

"It's all right. I can come in, can't I?"

"Yes. Sure. But you shouldn't stay wet."

"You mean I'll drip on everything?"

"I'll get you something to wear." He took the slicker from her and hung it in the smaller of the two bathrooms. He thought he'd find something for her to change into, but what? Everything he owned was far too big; Dan's clothing was even larger. Wait! What about those tan corduroys that boy had left here last summer? Dan's little friend.

He found the pants in the guest room closet, shook them out, sized them up. When he returned to the foyer, she had found the mop and was mopping up the floor.

"It looked so bright in here, from my place," she said, still explaining. "I don't know. So hospitable. You're sure I'm not intruding?"

"It's all the candles," he explained. "Dan buys them by the gross. Here, these are clean. I don't know who they belong to. Change and come warm up by the fire."

"You mean I can stay?"

He suddenly felt as though he were in a Pinter play where the delivery boy stops by, has a cup of tea, and doesn't leave for thirty years.

"Go change," he said, pointing to the guest room. "I'll get you something warm to drink."

Even the corduroys were too large, he saw when she came out; they hung on her, but she'd belted them tightly around her small waist, and they looked sort of charming, like rather thick harem bloomers.

"I won't forget this," she said.

He handed her a hot rum toddy he'd made. She sipped at it cautiously.

"Not too fast," he warned. "It's strong."

He led her into the big room and offered her his seat, but she remained standing by the fireplace, looking around, warming her legs, sipping her drink. Her hair was in one thick, long braid tonight. It glowed in the candle- and firelight. Her skin was so clear and bright it was like the skin on a pale-colored plum at its August ripest.

"I'm so glad you weren't working or anything," she said, then squatted down on the floor between the fireplace and where he sat. "I would have hated myself for interrupting you."

"Too much noise to work," he said. She certainly made herself at home quickly enough. Dear Abby, he thought, my neighbor's daughter came to visit me one stormy night and now she won't go home. What should I do to let her know I don't want her living here? Signed, Polite but perplexed. "You were there alone?" he asked to make conversation.

"Two days," she said. "I'm staying all week." Then she giggled. "If I can make it. Last night I was frightened because it was so incredibly quiet here with no cars and only the surf. Tonight I was scared because it was so stormy. I guess I'm just not a pioneer woman type, am I?"

Her voice was amazingly like her brother's, though higher pitched, even when she spoke low, like now. The way she rushed at her words at the beginning of a sentence, then slowed down at the end, was like him. How her a's were broad, not at all like a New Yorker's, more like a New Englander's. The facial resemblance was strong too, the clear-cut nose, the deep-set eyes, high cheekbones, the large forehead. The bottom half differed, however. Jerry's face was square, almost too square. His chin almost too wide, dimpled twice. His lips, especially his lower lip, were large too, as though to fill in all that space. Not hers. Her face, her chin were nicely pointed. Her mouth was small, fitting the smaller oval of her face, the smaller nose.

"I suppose you have the right to know why I'm out here all alone," she suddenly announced in a deeper voice, as though imitating someone older: her mother?

The last thing Jonathan wanted was the confessions of a frightened teenaged girl. "That's not necessary," he said, as calmly as possible.

Her gray eyes opened wide; he could see they were flecked with different colors: blue, gold, brown. Then she lowered them to gaze at the steaming mug in her lap.

"I guess you're right. It's not necessary."

"You're Sally," he said.

"Stevie!" She looked up. "It's really Stephanie, but somehow they began calling me 'Stevie' and it stuck. I wasn't a tomboy."

That explained the confusion. Dan always thought the reference Paula Locke made to Stevie was to another, younger brother: one unseen, and thus even more desirable than the deliciously known Jerry.

"And you're Jonathan Lash, the famous composer," she said.

"Hardly famous."

"More famous than anyone else I've ever met." Her eyes searched the room. Looking for signs of his fame? The scrolled honors, the autographed photos? "You know," she said, "I'm such a jerk sometimes. Here I am talking as though I were across the street or something, and your lover is probably trying to get to sleep."

"He's not here. He's in London, directing some films for the BBC."

Her eyebrows rose and fell; he read this as surprise, and/or being impressed.

"And no," he went on, "you aren't interrupting me at all. No intrusion. No bother. I'm sort of glad to have company."

"I tried playing solitaire," she said, then bit her upper lip, and fell silent, looking down at her mug.

Conversation lapsed. The rain still thundered overhead, lightning frequently brightened up behind the curtained windows, unpredictably, now on one side of the large room, now another; the fire settled, crackled, popped.

"May I tell you"—she suddenly looked up at him, as though begging, and embarrassed to be doing so—"may I tell you why I'm out here alone? I'd like to."

Jonathan didn't know how to respond. Good Lord, no! he thought, but nodded yes.

"I was supposed to be in college yesterday. Second year. I'm supposed to get engaged next month to a boy I've been seeing. And I don't want to. Isn't that strange? I don't want to go back to school, and I don't want to get married. I'm having a crisis. It's all very adolescent and typical of me that it's happening now, at eighteen, instead of when I was thirteen, like everyone else. An identity crisis,

I suppose it's called. So I came out here to be alone, to think, to make some clear-headed decisions about my life."

She sighed and sat back when she was done, relieved at having gotten it out.

The last part made up for the first part, which he hadn't at all wanted to hear. At least she was doing it independently, and didn't want his help.

"I see," he said.

"Well, I haven't done any of it," she said. "All I've done is read a mystery, lie in the sun, get tan, and then get scared and act like some kind of screwball tonight."

Jonathan suspected that was someone else talking for her: her parents, her teachers.

"The week isn't up yet," he said.

She smiled. "You're right! It isn't, is it? Why am I already admitting defeat?"

"Five more days left," he said.

"Sunny ones, I hope." Then, "You see, I was right to barge in here the way I did. I feel better already. An objective outsider is always best in these matters. Rose was right about that. I can't tell you how gloomy and damp it was over there. It's so nice here," she added, slung over a hassock now, and turned to look at the fire.

Well, that was easy, he thought. No complete confessions and suffering stories faced him now. He'd said exactly the right words to forestall them.

"I really love fires," she said. "They seem to have lives of their own, don't they?"

He looked at the fire. Underneath the two logs was a silver red white ashy furnace, as glitzy as a gay theme party decorated on the idea of Dante's *Inferno*. But it was lovely here, fitting.

He wanted to ask her questions: about Jerry, about her parents, her boyfriend, her school, her life. Dan would. Dan would never forgive him if he didn't use this opportunity. If Dan were here, he'd be pumping her for every shred of information, every detail of the Lockes' life that he'd wondered about in the seven years they'd been neighbors in Sea Mist. But Jonathan couldn't bring himself even to begin.

She yawned, stifled it, looked back at him apologetically, began to say something, then yawned again and shook her head, as though to clear it.

"The rum," he suggested. "Tired?"

"I didn't think I was," she said.

"Want to go to bed?" he said, and immediately regretted it.

She seemed to hear no implications in the offer. She only yawned again, like a sleepy child. "I can just lie down here by the fire. Don't trouble yourself."

"We have a guest room." Then, as she was beginning to doze against the hassock, he leaned toward her, touched her shoulder. She barely responded. So he helped her up, and along the corridor.

"I'll be all right," she said sleepily, as he led her into the guest room. Jonathan felt as he did with Artie and Ken, Dan's boys, whenever they'd stayed up too late, and had to be put to bed.

"There are some old pajamas in here," he said, opening the bureau drawer. A candle was burning in a dish on the night table next to the bed. "Don't forget to blow it out," he reminded her.

"Can I keep it on?" she asked. And now she really reminded him of the boys. "In case I wake up in the night."

"Sure. 'Night."

"Thanks. Thanks for taking in an orphan of the storm," she said, and waved weakly at him, a movement that was stopped in mid-gesture by a huge yawn.

He went back into the living room and decided to put on another few logs, to take the dampness out of the house. Then he made another rum toddy for himself, and finally sat down, drink in hand, cigarettes handy, to read that biography he'd brought out in June and still had not gotten to.

Oddly, he felt he could concentrate better now: even feel content. The rain was no less fierce, the thunder and lightning only a bit less tempestuous. Yet he did feel content. Was it knowing someone else was in the house with him? Often, after he and Dan had gone to bed and made love, and Dan had fallen asleep, he'd gotten dressed again and come out here to work, or to read, or just to sit out on the lounge chairs on the deck, hearing the ocean, looking up at the starry skies, thinking. It always felt better being awake this late, knowing someone else was sleeping.

He had to laugh when he thought what the consequences would be if her parents—especially Lady Bracknell—knew where their daughter was sleeping tonight.

What a pretty girl she was, though: nothing artificially pretty about her. Refreshing too, as youth was supposed to be for those older.

He felt much older now: almost as though he were her parent. Her mood swings were really extraordinary—from tears to placidity in a few minutes, from vivacity to exhaustion in another minute, from seeming indifference and poise to girlish confidentiality. Perhaps that really was what changed as one aged: one's moods evened out more. One had longer stretches of each—days of contentment, weeks of boredom, months of depression, years of satisfaction. He might use these sudden changes of temperament of Stevie's in a song or two in *Lady and the Falcon,* to display Fiammetta's youthfulness. She was only sixteen or so in the story, wasn't she? All those quattrocento girls married early.

The biography sat in his lap with a weight that was in itself a reproach. But he didn't even open it. He was thinking about Fiammetta in Florence, and how her music would be more youthful, more truthful now.

CHAPTER SIX

At first she thought she was in the berth of a large ocean liner, sailing in the middle of the Mediterranean. The sky, through the gauzy curtains on three sides, was an intense, cloudless blue. Even with the curtains closed, the room was so bright she had to close her eyes again.

When she opened them she knew where she was—the guest bedroom of the lovers' house. She remembered last night, and how she'd arrived here, but she didn't recall anything of what had happened after her arrival; she had been so relieved, so suddenly exhausted. She vaguely remembered that one lover was away in Europe, and that the other had been surprised, reserved, helpful yet distant from her, however cordial.

She wondered if he were up yet. She had to get up. She couldn't just lie here. Not with that sky, that sun! She had to get up, whether he was awake or not.

The corduroys she'd worn last night were on the table next to the bed, along with a gutted candle in a dish.

What a nice room this was. The curtains, once pulled, revealed the rich wine-colored carpeting, a half wall of closets in rosewood, built in with shelves, stereo equipment, a color television, even a little pull-out desk or vanity with its own telephone. The other door led to a bathroom—sleek, contemporary in its fixtures and accessories, very no-nonsense in brown and beige, complementing the decor of the bedroom. And outside—well, with the curtains opened all around, the bedroom seemed to float on a little wooden deck, in the middle of a wood—a hidden little cove, a private place for sitting, sunning, even for making love in the afternoon.

She pulled on her T-shirt and the corduroys and stepped out onto the deck. The sun was hot, so strong it had burnt the rain off the leaves, dried off the decking. Under the bushes the dark wet ground steamed as though in a tropical jungle. She realized this was the direction of her family's house, which she could just make out through the foliage. Were there other little hidden terraces like this one? she wondered. She thought she had seen the entire house last summer at the lovers' party. Wouldn't this be a lovely spot to sun in.

Back in the bedroom, she left a glass door open to air out the room. Then she found her sneakers and sweatshirt and peeked out into the corridor. It was empty: one door at the end open a few inches; that must be the lovers' bedroom. He must be awake.

But there was no one in the kitchen, or dining room—an area surrounded on two sides with glass, a raised skylight overhead, garden on one side, the ocean view on the other—nor was there anyone in the large central room where they'd sat and talked last night. The place seemed far larger than she remembered.

She found her slicker still hanging in the little bathroom off the foyer. Next to the fireplace, her denims were hung, dry. She changed into them, then went around opening up curtains and doors to air out the slightly dense, nutty odor of the dead fireplace. Outside the living area was a three-quarters surrounding deck that dropped a level to a lower, larger deck, from which in turn, paths led to the beach. Even the white sand looked hot and dry.

Back inside, she crept down the hallway to the last door and opened it a few inches more.

Jonathan was still sleeping. His room was steaming hot. He'd pulled off most of his bedclothes already. He was rolled over on one side, away from her, the sheets twisted around his body. She whispered his name, hoping he would be awake enough to hear. No reaction. She tried again, a bit louder, trying to thank him and to tell him she was going now.

He was sound asleep. Well, she couldn't remain here all day waiting for him to wake up. She'd come back and thank him later.

The room was too hot. Like the one she'd slept in, it faced east, though more southerly. It too had its private deck, but this one opened onto the ocean. She slid open the glass door, hoping it wouldn't make noise. It didn't. Then she slid open the door opposite. That was better, cooler. He'd sleep more comfortably now.

She closed the bedroom door, exactly as she had found it, and left the house. With its doors open, its curtains flapping in the wind, it reminded her somehow of a house in a Fellini movie she'd once seen.

Almost back at her family's house, she had an idea—she would change into cooler clothing and make Jonathan some coffee. He didn't usually sleep late, she recalled. He'd been awake yesterday morning before her, already composing on the oceanside deck, when she'd wandered out. And in previous summers, the lovers were ordinarily up early: on their deck, on the beach, going into the little village for groceries, the mail, a morning newspaper.

Problem number one was that there was no coffee in her kitchen. Her mother must have packed it away and carried it into the city. And she did so want coffee. Only one solution: she would go into the village and buy a can. Inside her family's house, she went around opening windows and doors to the bright hot day. How different it looked after last night's terrors. How tiny and shoddy and crowded with old beach furniture, after the lovers' house. How shy the little fireplace seemed; how inadequate the hurricane lamp on the table; how sad the deck of playing cards still spread out in mid-game next to the paperback mystery. The whole place looked apologetic; as though it had failed her and knew it. "Dear old place," she said aloud, forgiving it, reminding herself that after all, it was her parents' house, and how much could she really expect from it?

"'Bye," she said, when she left to head toward the village, as though someone were in the house to answer. After only a few steps, she stopped. Wait a minute. The lovers must have coffee in their house. She'd make it there.

Their house still seemed empty, although it was cooler now.

She found coffee all right—more of it than she knew what to do with. Plastic containers of coffee were stacked up in the corner of a counter, each type carefully marked in felt tip ink: Mocha Java, French Blend, African Koola, Colombian, Brazilian. Problem number two was that all of them were whole coffee beans and had to be ground to be used. She located the grinder, plugged it into a wall socket, and prayed she wasn't doing something wrong. It worked. Fine. Now for a coffeepot. She was in and out of cabinets before she noticed—on the counter, naturally, where she'd passed it a dozen times—the large Chemex drip coffeemaker. Now to select a blend. Several of them sounded fine, but as she was used to already canned blends, she wasn't certain which was which. How about the French Blend? That sounded like a morning coffee to her, with its intimations of repasts at café tables surrounded by trees pinkly in bloom, and accompanied by a little tray of brioches and jams. She ground the coffee, boiled the water, poured the blend into the filter, added the water, wishing something here had instructions, so she could know if she were doing it right.

It was easy to guess men worked in this kitchen; it was so technical, so up-to-date with its hanging graduated copper bowls, its various measuring cups lined up, its stacks of plastic containers, its blenders, juicers, toasters, and broilers. A little army of knives of all shapes and sizes greeted her with military cleanliness in one corner. At the opposite end of the counter were a more frolicsome grouping of utensils—potato parers and slotted spoons, and a variety of wooden, steel, and plastic implements only half of which she'd ever seen before. All of them in order, all of them visible. It reminded her of her father's workshop at home.

The coffee turned out scrumptiously good when she tasted it. Perhaps there was something to taking this much trouble over it.

She thought she heard mumbling, and looked down the hall toward his bedroom. Through the doorspace, she could see the sheets moving. He must finally be waking up.

She poured a second cupful, found a sugar bowl and matching creamer, spoons, and a lovely brown lacquered tray to hold it all. Wouldn't he be surprised? Carrying it to the bedroom, she felt like the butler to a great financier in his summer palazzo on Lake Locarno. She wished she had today's newspaper to set on the tray.

"Good morning, sir!" she greeted him, entering the room and looking around for a place to set down the tray near his bed. "And it is a beautiful day, too, after last night's storm!" Her words trailed away.

Jonathan was half sitting up in bed, against the pillows, the sheets down to his ankles. His skin was honey tan against the pale blue sheets, amazingly solid against their crinkled fine flatness. One of his arms was thrown up over his rumpled curly brown hair. His mouth was half open, his lower teeth and his tongue visible. His eyes were only half-opened too.

Stevie stopped still, looking, or rather letting her eyes look, take photographs for her mind; otherwise she felt utterly blank, utterly filled up at the same time by what she was seeing, so that she couldn't think, couldn't speak, couldn't move, couldn't do anything but look. Look at how his dark fine body hair encircled each tiny cinnamon-colored nipple of his well-defined chest, then sloped in together to meet in a single line inches below on a little ridge of bone—his sternum—from there to slide and furrow and cascade over muscled ripples down to the flat plain of his paler lower groin, where the line of hair spread again, bushing thickly around his genitals—his half-erect penis, tilted up toward his navel—as the dark hair spread again, under his scrotum to softly cover the tops of his thighs, and to finally, eventually, disappear into his tanned calves.

"Oh! Coffee," she heard him say, and she looked back up his length from the tangled sheets to his face again. "You made coffee. How nice," he said. He smiled sleepily at Stevie, and gestured toward her.

She felt as though she were about to freeze to death. No, that wasn't precisely right. Her arms and legs felt prickled, as though with a sudden rash, as though the nerve endings had all short-circuited at once, declaring a neural emergency. It was worse, different in her lower torso; her stomach seemed to be burning, yet at the same time to be involuntarily contracting and expanding so quickly, so forcefully she thought she was about to urinate.

"You can put the tray down here," he was saying, "on the bed." He reached up for it, took the tray out of her hands, and set it down on the sheets.

The freezing, burning, and other sensations in her body seemed to meet and flow together, gushing, and Stevie thought, Oh, my God, now I've done it.

"Sit down," he said. She went to a nearby armchair, and was about to sit, satisfied at least that her legs were working. But he motioned her over to the edge of the bed. "Isn't this cup for you? Or do I get both?"

She sat on the edge of the bed, facing away from him. That wouldn't do. She looked down to check if her shorts were soaked— and was surprised that they weren't. What could it have been? She still felt odd, still felt that prickling sensation in her lower torso, still felt blankness, even panic. It was something of a relief that she didn't have to be embarrassed over incontinence too. She turned to face him.

"I really need this," he sighed. Then, after a few sips, "You sleep well?"

She didn't answer: she was too busy staring at him again, sweeping once more from his ankles to his face. He suddenly realized something was wrong.

"Jesus! How stupid of me," he said, and reached down to cover himself with the sheet. "Sorry. Guess I wasn't thinking too clearly."

"That's all right," she managed to say in a small, deceptively calm voice. "You don't have to," she added, then lied, "I'm used to it." She had to stop her hand from reaching up and uncovering his body. Looking at it had somehow set off all these reactions in herself, she knew, and while it was definitely strange and uncomfortable, she didn't want it to end: not yet. "You don't have to cover up in front of me."

"Well?" He hesitated. "If you say so." Still, he didn't uncover himself. He wasn't really convinced. She felt she had to say something else, in defense.

"I do have a boyfriend, you know," she said, and was now

amazed by how blasé she could be. "And this isn't nineteen fifty-three, is it?"

"I suppose not," he said, but looked puzzled, and she wondered what in the world had prompted her to choose that year.

"I'm never sure anymore what is allowed and what isn't with younger people," he replied.

She turned away from him and stared into the depths of the coffee mug. No relief there: the coffee, with cream, was precisely the color of his abdomen. She sighed.

"You didn't have to go to all the bother of making coffee," he said. "I do appreciate it, however."

"I got up early."

Her voice continued to lie blithely past her emotions, and little by little, she began to believe she could even make small talk with him, sitting here, on the edge of his bed, with him so close, his body so present, and she would get away with it—fool him and herself.

But could she ever reveal what she was really thinking to him? Or to anyone? How she'd seen Bill Tierney naked a dozen times, ditto her brother, and even a few other men; and although they were all certainly as attractive as any girl could desire, she'd never felt like this. Would Jonathan understand that? What was it, anyway, about him that had done it? Was it his position on the bed as she had come in the room, lying so thoughtlessly, so luxuriously among the tangle of sheets and the plump pillows? Was it the color of his skin—so honey brown—against the ice blue of the bedclothes? His sleepy vulnerability? Whatever it was, it had given her a brand-new experience, set off a chain reaction of little explosions that had culminated in her vagina—she had to admit it now—that no man or boy, even her crushes, even her rock star idols hadn't come near before.

Jonathan stretched again. This time she noticed that his underarm was amazingly vanilla-white against the darkness of the hair there, and the deep tan of his skin. She had to force herself to look away.

"I think I'm finally beginning to come around," he said.

Why had she never noticed before what a handsome face he

had? His eyes were large and brown and deep. His eyelashes were long, curled—an effect most women required mascara to achieve, but his were natural, uncosmetized. The black stubble in those areas of his bearded cheek and neck that he shaved was so regularly spaced as to seem deliberately placed. Even the gray hairs that stood out among the more frequent black of his mustache appeared to have been spliced in specifically for her admiration.

"What's on your agenda today?" he asked. "Going to try to work on that crisis of yours? Or just read and sun?"

Now she remembered last night. And to think she had been fool enough then to have wanted to confide in him about Bill. That would have been the kiss of death. Thank God, she hadn't. Or rather, thank God, he'd had the sense not to let her.

"Probably tanning and reading. You?"

"I don't know. I'll work a bit. Maybe take a swim."

Perhaps this was what people spoke of when they talked of love at first sight, Stevie thought. And yet, it wasn't exactly first sight, was it? More as though her eyes had suddenly been opened: enlightenment. Hadn't it been Saint Augustine who had written about that? And, she had to admit, it wasn't really love either— although it could easily turn into that. It was lust, absolute, pure sexual desire that had swept her body and was plaguing her still, though diminishing somewhat. But it must have been something else too: some emotion; because while she wanted more than anything to stay here, next to him, with a good view of him, she also knew that if she remained here another minute she'd do something awful, scream, break into tears, attack him.

"Well," she said, as calmly as before, "I guess I'll be going then." She stood up.

"Leave the tray."

"I'll take it."

He was so unconscious of her presence, they hardly were in the same room together. She picked up the tray, and he didn't protest, but continued to sip his coffee and look up slightly questioningly at her. "What?" he finally asked.

Now she was in a fix. She got control of her tongue after some time and said, "Thank you."

"For last night? Don't be silly. I'm glad you felt enough trust to come over."

"That's not all," she began, then stopped herself. She wanted to thank him for her new experience, her new knowledge of herself: to thank him for being tanned and manly and naked and almost but not quite erect, for being sleepy and for having such long eyelashes, and for merely being.

Instead, she said good-bye and fled the house.

She ran down to the surf, and still wearing her shorts and T-shirt, plunged into the tide.

Chapter Seven

"Mind if I sit down?" Jonathan asked. He looked down the length of the beach one way—empty—then the other way, also empty except for Mrs. Perle's umbrella in the distance, the little soda-shop table and chairs set out as usual, with Giorgio and Ricotta, the old lady's silent companions, propped up as though they'd had too much to drink.

Stevie turned over and looked up at him. He wasn't sure whether she was frowning or merely trying to see who he was in the glare of the sunlight. He hadn't meant to startle her.

"I promise I won't interfere with your reading," he offered.

"It's nothing great." She'd been on her stomach. She turned around and sat up, making room for him on the large navy blue towel. "Just something I found in the house." She gestured for him to sit. He did, cross-legged, and inspected the book's broken-spined title.

"*The Devil's Third Eye.* Sounds scary."

"Not really." She seemed so shy now, so reticent that Jonathan wondered again if his impulse to stop and sit here with her had been a mistake. He'd been drawn to her—here on the desolate stretch of rough sand the storm last night had furrowed and carved—by her presence, by the presence of some life on the otherwise dead beach.

"Look," he said, "if I'm disturbing you or anything…"

"No." A small smile from her. She'd already gotten good

coloring in the few days she'd been here. Her smooth young face glowed with it.

"You did say you had a lot of thinking to do."

"I know. I'm sorry."

"For what?"

"For laying all that on you."

"But you didn't. Here," he said, "don't frown. Thanks for the coffee this morning. I really needed it. Sorry I wasn't better company for you. I'm not any good until at least an hour after I've awakened."

She looked even more distressed at this remark. Had she really been upset by his nakedness? Why had he stupidly thought she was Dan this morning? Lady Bracknell would have had a fit if she'd been there.

"I'll keep quiet," he said. "Go on reading." He handed her the book.

She took it, and he stretched out on his back, his hands beneath his head as a pillow.

Another splendid sunny day. After that insane storm. What did these sudden changes of weather portend, anyway? Change of the seasons, naturally. Spring coming with rain. Autumn too. "Rowdy weather," Dan called it. He hated it.

He'd seemed distant on the telephone this morning. Distant and quite excited too. The flat in Chelsea had central heating and a shower, Dan reported. Very American, Dan said, already using a British accent. He would be impossibly, archly British for months after he returned. Dan was always affected by accents and speech patterns, when he traveled. After the Los Angeles trip, he'd bought roller skates because he'd loved skating along the boardwalks in Venice. Even though Jonathan and all the rest of their friends had laughed at him and none had joined him, Dan had gone out on the streets with the damn things, grocery shopping, tooling along the bike paths in Central Park. He'd even spoken like an Angeleno. His ex-wife, Janet, had counted eight uses of the word "karma" in one evening's conversation with Dan. And what had Jonathan done with his beautiful self last night? Dan asked, always on the alert for infidelity, although he was the one who encouraged it, used it as a justification for his own philandering, calling it part of their open relationship.

Nothing, Jonathan told him: it had rained like the end of the world in a Japanese horror movie. Of course Dan was hardly interested. He sailed into a paean on British boys. Not even there one night—and already. How gorgeous they really were, Jonathan, at least at the age of twenty or so. They began falling apart by twenty-five, got pasty-faced and fat, or lean and bony. Dan would have some British boys to report on soon; perhaps he'd even have a little affair there. Unlikely, too much work to do. Daniel...

"What?" he said, aloud, only just aware that she'd said something to him.

"You can take off your shorts, if you want," she said. "You know, to get evenly tanned. I don't mind."

What? he thought. What? "No. That's all right. Besides, I'm not evenly tanned."

"I know." She'd put down the book and was leaning on one elbow. "Go on, don't mind me."

She was flirting, wasn't she? Or was she mocking him? He couldn't be certain which. Her eyes didn't give her away: they were steady and gray—a little darker in this strong sunlight—almost blue.

"I only do that in the privacy of my bedroom," he said, "with unmarried young ladies present."

She smiled and turned away, putting her head down. "Besides! What would Lady Bracknell say, if she knew I was corrupting her teenaged daughter?"

"Lady Bracknell?" Her head jerked up.

"That's what Dan calls your mother. You know, after the Oscar Wilde character."

He had no idea how she would react. He wasn't prepared for what she did, however. Putting one slender finger up to her lips, she seemed to think rather seriously, then said, "It's Lord Bracknell. My dad. My mom's all right. *He's* the one!"

Then she began to giggle.

"She *would* have gone into contortions, though," Stevie said, not hiding her amusement, "if she'd seen us. Especially if she knew…"

She stopped herself, then said in a conspiratorial voice, "Especially if she knew what happened to me this morning."

"What did happen to you?"

"I had a hot flash."

"A what?"

"A hot flash. You know, something sexual." Now she was a little girl, maybe eleven or twelve, giggling and refusing to explain.

"A hot flash," she said again, more calmly. "At least I think that's what women call it."

She *was* flirting with him. He decided to defuse it.

"Is that anything like a fat attack? You know, when you absolutely have to eat a pint of chocolate ice cream?"

"Close," she said. "No. Not close at all." And now she was twenty-eight or so, Nurse Locke, analytical and calm. "It's a physiological thing. They only call it a hot flash in trashy magazines. I suppose it's something like when a man has a spontaneous emission. You know, without him even being aware he's aroused."

Jonathan didn't know whether it was her calmness or what her words meant, but he was feeling uncomfortable. What was it with these kids anyway that allowed them to talk so openly about these matters? Thinking fast, he asked: "Who's Rose?"

"Rose Heywood?" she asked.

"I guess."

"She teaches history of ideas courses at school. She's a friend of mine. Why?"

"Nothing. You mentioned her last night."

Her face closed up again; so he decided to keep on the attack. "Look, I'm sorry about being so indifferent to your need to confide in someone last night. It was very rude of me. If there's anything you feel you need to discuss…"

"No." The smile again—deceptive little smile, what did it signify? "No. It's okay." She felt the need to explain. "To me that would be a worse breach of taste than serving you coffee in bed unexpectedly this morning."

"I appreciated that."

"I should have known better than to intrude."

"You didn't."

"You thought I was someone else."

"I was half asleep."

"I know. All tangled in the sheets."

"Cotton-mouthed and foul-tempered," he put in.

"Rumpled and funny-looking," she said. She looked down at the paperback. "This book is terrible."

"We've got shelvesful," he said. "Why not come sometime and browse? Dan reads like an addict, and I do some too." Then he had a thought: What did she read, anyway? What did eighteen-year-old girls read nowadays? *Madame Bovary*? Virginia Woolf? Gothic novels? "What kind of books do you read?"

"All kinds."

She was playing with him again. Reveal and hide. Speak out, then be secretive. She *was* flirting. She was evidently pleased about this morning—not upset as he had thought at first. Somehow it gave her an imagined power over him—equalized them in some way in her mind. Whatever else Stevie Locke might be, she wasn't a fool, that was certain. Perhaps a little too smart. No wonder she was having an identity crisis. Didn't she know—hadn't she learned by now—that intelligence was as much a wound as an aid in life?

"Okay," he said, playing, "what was the last book you read?"

"The Devil's Third Eye." Complete with the smile again.

"Before that?"

"Phillip Aries's *Centuries of Childhood.*"

"Well! That's too fancy for me. Perhaps we don't have anything on our shelves to interest you."

"I was teasing," she said, looking him in the eyes. She liked this game. He wondered if she were lying about this morning too—about her spontaneous orgasm or whatever it was—trying to get a rise out of him, to make him feel uncomfortable. "I did read it for a course I took last year. I hadn't had time to read it during the semester."

Jonathan heard shouting and turned away from her to look in the direction it seemed to come from. Two tall, flat-bodied boys wearing full-length black rubber surfing suits were rushing out into the waves, their long slender surfboards tilted in the sand on shore. Even from here, Jonathan knew them—the Halley boys, sons of the liquor store proprietor.

"Looks like we have company," he said.

"Not much," she replied, and turned onto her stomach after a cursory glance at them.

"The older one's terrific-looking," Jonathan said. Now he was gaming with her, trying to make her feel uncomfortable.

He expected her to turn over, inspect them, then comment. She didn't. Instead she said, "He's a cracker. They both are."

"That's what Dan calls them too. But for Dan that increases their attractiveness."

"Not for me."

"Doesn't your boyfriend have that kind of body? Tall, wide-shouldered, small-hipped, flat-chested, all-American boy?"

"I suppose," she said, not very enthusiastically.

"He's on the shit list this week, huh?"

She laughed. "He sure is." She rolled over on her side, facing him, slim, lithe, bikini-clad, and reached out as though stretching, with her hands and feet. She looked like a kitten on its back playing with a ball of yarn. "Bill and Lord and Lady Bracknell are *all* on the shit list."

"How about Jerry?" Jonathan asked, hoping this would make up for his discretion last night, and so, eventually, satisfy Dan's insatiable need for knowledge about past crushes.

Mock dismay from her. "Jerry's a lost cause. Lobotomized."

"Are you friends with him?"

"Not really. Not anymore. Do you have brothers and sisters?" she suddenly asked in a different voice, sitting up and serious again, quite studentlike. "I never even thought of that before. I wonder why not?" She pondered, then seemed to frown again. "Just goes to show you how you can't escape parents even when they're not around, doesn't it? I think that all this while I assumed you and Dan only had each other, only *could* have each other. No brothers, sisters, family, apart from each other. Damn! How could I think otherwise, with all that brainwashing."

Jonathan wanted to ask what kind of brainwashing. What had her parents said about him and Dan? He guessed he didn't really want to know; didn't care. But she was something else, more interesting by far than he had expected. Obviously she was at the point in her young life when she was questioning everything—all her assumptions, teachings, values. It was something Dan often did—maddeningly at times. But Stevie seemed quieter about it: deeper too. What a pleasure to be able to sense an active mind behind that very pretty face so young it seemed to be blank most of the time. If only her eyes didn't have that glossy freshness of childhood too.

"And Jerry?" he asked.

"He's interning."

"That doesn't sound too desperate."

"For him it is."

"You think he'll make a bad doctor?"

"No. He'll be fine. Capable. He'll have an enormous, mostly female practice in a few years, and he'll live very comfortably off mastectomy referrals and diet pill prescriptions, and afternoon office adulteries."

"That doesn't sound too terrible a life for a man," he said.

"You're all alike," she said wearily.

"Not me! I don't exploit any women. I even have a male cleaning woman."

"Do you fuck around much when Dan's away?" she asked.

Wow! That came out of left field.

"Do you?" he asked back.

"I'm not married," she said, "and don't say you're not. It's the same thing."

"Did you know that Dan had the hots for your brother?"

"I know."

"Really. How?"

"Jerry told me. He said he would probably have done it with Dan too, but he never had the time. He thought Dan was sweet."

"Wait till I tell Dan. He'll reserve a seat on the next plane back."

"Jerry told me that Dan was much nicer to him than most of the women out here, and that's why he would sleep with him. To show how grateful he was. He said that Dan had no expectations either. I guess that's what it all comes down to, doesn't it?"

"Lack of expectations?" he asked. He'd lost her.

"That too," she said. "No, being…being human."

He had the urge to touch her, and did, on her hot, smooth shoulder. "You shouldn't worry too much. You seem to have it all in place."

She looked at him with a question, but didn't ask it.

He took his hand off her, and she intercepted it and held it next to her own, then turned it over, palm up.

"Look at all the lines on my hand, compared to yours," he said.

They compared palms silently, his square with large tufts of flesh, the long, straight fingers, slightly knobby at the joints; hers finer, oval-shaped, flat, with slender tapering fingers. She had a tiny scar between the two middle fingers.

She touched his gold ring. "Did Dan give you this?"

"Stevie," he suddenly said, surprising himself, but feeling incredibly sympathetic with her plight. "I'm on your side."

"Thanks. I know that. You and Rose are. I don't know if that's enough."

"If you're on your side too that's all you need," he said.

"I wish Lord Bracknell thought that," she said sadly.

"Fuck Lord Bracknell."

A surprised look from her, then a mischievous smile. "Would you?"

He had to think. He tried to picture Vernon Locke, tried to remember him objectively. He was older, of course: out of shape. But not bad.

"Would you?" he asked.

She squeezed his hand between hers. "I asked first."

He pretended to ponder. He liked having her hold his hand and look at him, liked this little game with her. "In a pinch," he finally said. "And you?"

"In a pinch," she agreed, then let go of his hand and began to laugh so hard she fell backward on the beach blanket. When she could speak clearly again, she said, "Lord Bracknell is right! You *are* corrupting me. Thank God! I was *so* bored!"

She looked up at him, comfortable on the blanket. He was reminded of years ago, when he was in high school, when he and a girl friend, Francine, had gone to the beach, on picnics and rides. They'd never done more than kissed and necked a little at a school dance; but they'd always amused each other, tested each other, kept each other sharp, satisfied each other's need for companionship. He wondered where Francine was now, and if she were happy.

Suddenly he felt as though something were expected of him: the way she was staring at him, appraising him almost. He stood up, shaking off the sand that had stuck to his legs.

"You want to come look at those books?" he offered.

"Another time," she said.

"Whenever."

"Wait!" She sat up. "I have an idea. Why don't you come to my place for dinner tonight?"

It was so spontaneously said, he answered, "Fine." Then, "Can you cook?"

"I'm a brilliant—although somewhat limited—cook."

"Limited how?"

"You'll see," she said. The smile again. "What time?"

"Eight? Nine?"

They agreed on nine.

"Should I bring anything? Wine? Bunches of dried leaves for your table setting?"

"Both," she said, jumping to her feet. He was glad he'd accepted her offer. She was already in the mood to do something about it. It would be fun for her. "I have to go shopping for food," she said, remembering something. "'Bye!" and she started off.

"Hey!" he called.

"What?" Turning back.

"Is this formal?" he asked.

"Don't come naked," she said, then turned again and ran up toward her house.

He watched her for a while until she had reached the oceanside deck, washed off her feet with a hose, then went in.

Jonathan sat back down on the beach towel and looked at the boys bathing in the surf. They had probably decided against surfing today; both had taken off their rubber suits and were diving and swimming, much closer now than before, brought down this end by the strong tide.

They were extraordinary, he thought. Awfully blond. What did teenaged girls know of male beauty? He couldn't get enough of them.

CHAPTER EIGHT

Everything was ready but the fish. That was slowly baking in the oven, according to her mother's recipe. Just before serving it, Stevie would cover it with a sauce and slip it under the broiler for a fast browning. Otherwise, everything was fine. The salad looked fresh and colorful in its transparent bowl; the cold asparagus were laid out accompanied by two little dishes of fresh mayonnaise; even the rice and pea mixture would be served cold. The table was placed by the windows onto the ocean deck, set for two, with the pale blue china her mother never used because it was too good for summer dining; the practical flatware shined to a glitter; two ceramic candlesticks found hidden in a closet. She hoped he wouldn't bring the dead leaves, as he had teased he would. She'd collected some late-blooming irises and long-stemmed willows from the garden of the Winstons' house, closed weeks ago.

She should have told him which wine he was to bring. The house looked fine, finally. She'd spent all afternoon on it, hiding the awful throw pillows, taking down the paintings on the walls, those awful "textured" seascapes her father had bought years ago in the city, because he thought they were appropriately marine. Lord Bracknell. That fitted him. Neither a monster nor a myth; wasn't that how Wilde characterized his character? That was Dad, all right.

Really, if Mother were here, she would see right off how much better the place looked with all that extra furniture stashed away in the shed under the house, the walls bare; the knickknacks packed away; those awful curtains down; the windows exposed. Maybe Stevie ought to go into decorating. No, too many fags.

She blushed then, looking in the mirror, applying her eyeshadow. Then she said out loud, "Idiot! What do you think Jonathan is?" and continued making up.

Of course she was out of her mind inviting him here for dinner. But then, what harm was there in it? She was merely being neighborly. Friendly. Repaying her social obligation to him. Even Lady Bracknell would have to agree with that.

"Inspection time!" she said, aloud.

Not bad. She'd gotten excellent color on the beach. What a beautiful day it had been, what a gorgeous sunset too! The very one she'd thought about on her arrival here in Sea Mist. The sun had become a huge, deep-red disk, flat on either tip, and had slowly sunk through layers of colored sky, each pastel more delicious and impossible than the next: fluffy magentas giving way to marbled pinks, in turn making way for sherbet oranges, followed by salmon mousses. Amid all these cool-hot colors had been one thin cloud—cirrus, she recalled, was its name—that had been an electric yellow. It had forked at one point to enclose an area of the sky untouched by the prevailing red spectrum—a satiny neon blue, like her brother Jerry's basketball shorts. Every second the colors shaded and transformed themselves into subtle new shifts of tint, layer by layer. Then she became aware of the sudden silence around her: the lack of wind, the sudden cessation of birdsong. It was as though the entire day suddenly sighed for a minute. Then, from behind her, she barely made out an approaching sound—the muffled, distant flapping of many large wings. In an instant they arrived—brownish gray, flying low over the housetops and pine trees, coordinated, in a loose V-shape—the geese!

That had been exquisite. The second exquisite moment of the day—a day not yet ended.

The first, of course, had been her discovery of Jonathan this morning. She'd felt that primarily as lust, but after she'd dashed into the ocean, she'd come back to the house and analyzed the surge into several layers of meaning. Uppermost was the new fact of her intense desire for a man—that man, where he was, as he was at that moment. That had never happened to her before, and it had overwhelmed her. She'd wanted to possess him: to caress him like a mother, and at the same time to cover his body with passionate bites and kisses, like a courtesan. Bill Tierney would never believe it was possible, even if she were stupid enough to ever tell him. He called Stevie the Ice Princess; and it wasn't always said jokingly. Not that she was frigid or anything awful like that. She simply had never felt that connected to physicality before. She had never really understood why it was that men and boys found her far more attractive than she ever found them, why they felt drawn to her when she could take them or leave them. Sometimes she thought it was a pose on their part, an affectation, or even worse, a merely mechanical working out of what they thought they ought to be doing and feeling around a halfway good-looking female: something men pretended without ever really feeling. She recalled how queasy she'd gotten one afternoon, on the sailboat with Bill out on the Long Island Sound, when she'd caught him looking at her with that stricken, fascinated, wounded look. It had given her the creeps. She'd certainly never expected to be on the other end of that bizarre an emotion.

Next, naturally, was the sensation—intuitive, yet no less strong for that—that she would do something, possibly a great deal, probably anything to sleep with Jonathan Lash. Despite the fact that he had a lover, was gay, was twice her age, and wasn't obviously interested in her. All those negatives made it more of an adventure. She desperately needed adventure. That was why she'd come out here alone, to test herself against the unknown—whatever that might be—if only to prove to herself she was still alive, still unlobotomized. Which scientific writer had she skimmed last term who'd written that the only certain proof that an organism was truly alive was its struggle to change the life and environment around it? She couldn't recall, but she certainly agreed.

Her face was done, her hair in two long barrettes, swept up behind her ears and down. The blouse and slacks she'd bought this afternoon at the harborside boutique looked really good. That had been a stroke of luck; she'd almost run past in her hurry to get dinner shopping done. Thank God, she could never bypass a sign that read, "Season Closing—Fifty Percent Off!" She had few enough clothes out here to begin with: nothing but denims and work shirts. But, then, who'd considered when she'd packed her bag that morning that she'd be doing this—having dinner with a man she wanted. It seemed that everything was conspiring to help her.

"Wicked woman," she said to her reflection. "Whore of Babylon." She pursed her lips. "I wish," she responded tartly.

It was nine o'clock. Where was he? Outside on the ocean deck it was dark, clear, starry, quite warm. She could see the lights from his house. What was he doing now, this minute? Getting dressed? Standing in that big bathroom, a towel wrapped around his hips, shaving, around his beard, trimming it, inspecting his face for tiny nicks? She hated not being there.

Faint steps on the boardwalk. He was coming.

The footsteps approached, and went past the entry to her family's house: someone walking to the beach.

It made no sense to just wait out here, agonizing. She ought to do something, check the fish, mix them drinks. What if he wanted a drink? Had they left any liquor in the house?

In the kitchen, she found a bottle of cooking sherry and a small flask of brandy—not a great brand either: for cooking too, she supposed.

"Hi! Anyone home?"

Calm yourself, Stevie. He's here.

She felt like a parody of her mother, sweeping graciously out of the kitchen to greet her guest.

He'd dressed as though for a garden party: beige open-necked shirt of some silky material, pale blue jacket, white pants pleated at the waist, cinctured with a thin beige belt, and white shoes. Tan, dark-haired and bearded, he looked smashing—like an oil sheikh's playboy son on the Riviera.

"I'm not too early, am I?"

"No, fine. Come in."

He held a bottle of white wine in one hand. Naturally. He would never—even unconsciously—do the wrong thing; she'd already expected that. He offered the bottle to her, label up.

"You didn't say white or red," he apologized.

"This looks exactly right," she said. He was still waiting in the doorway. "Please come in."

He did and she felt more comfortable.

"I just discovered we have almost nothing in the way of liquor," she said, hoping it was spontaneous. "So I can't offer you a drink. Should I chill this?"

"Serve cool," he said, looking around the living room.

She couldn't recall if he'd ever been inside the house before. His scrutiny made her edgy: as though he were evaluating her through the house. She hoped not.

"It looks different," he said. "Nice."

"Not like your place," she said, but felt relieved. It was the simplicity and rich texturing of the lovers' house that had inspired her own patchwork redecoration. "Correction on the drinks. We have sherry and a little brandy."

"Soda? Tonic? Lemon?"

"Yes. I think so."

"Good. I'll throw together a brandy cocktail I know how to make. Everyone eventually ends up drinking the cooking sherry, you know."

"This is delicious," she said a few moments later, sipping the tall, fresh drink. "What's it called?"

"Brandy and tonic, I guess. The British drank it in the Orient, to ward off malaria."

She led him out onto the deck, where he held his drink up and tapped its rim against her glass.

"To your decision."

They clinked glasses again.

"You don't even know what my decision is yet," she said. "I don't think I do either."

"No. But I support it. Whatever it is."

Earlier in the afternoon, Stevie had pictured this very moment: the two of them here on the deck, having cocktails before dinner, the

Milky Way stretched across the sky above them, the soft pounding of the surf. Several times while thinking of this moment she had panicked, wondering what they would talk about. Today, on the beach, hadn't been a particularly illustrious beginning, she thought.

But there was no problem. At ease here, as he must be anywhere, it seemed, Jonathan immediately began to speak of Sea Mist and its residents. He'd spent several full summers here, and seemed to know the people of the resort far more fully than she or her parents. He talked about the community, the ecology of the island, with a sense of pride and an evident pleasure that made her regret having only perceived it as a beach. Jonathan seemed to know everything about Sea Mist. He knew the various birds and flowers, the incredibly varied insect life. He knew which buds on which bushes opened in May or June, which insects were attracted to their blooms, what week the flowers fell and the leaves began to turn, which birds passed over them migrating south. He'd revived birds that had flown into plate glass windows and doors, had seen those very birds return later on in the summer, and then, the following summer with their families. He'd nursed back to health during the early spring cats and dogs lost out here the summer before, who'd managed somehow to survive the brutal island winters. He knew all the constellations wheeling majestically overhead, and as he pointed them out, he could make Stevie see terribly clearly for the first time in her life why they were called Archer, Whale, Swan.

Over dinner, he continued talking—about the history of Sea Mist from its earliest days as a lookout station for shipwrecks, to the free port era in the middle half of the nineteenth century, when the China trade clippers dropped half or more of their cargo here, hiding it until it could be transported across the bay. Then they sailed into New York Harbor, where they naturally paid much lighter duties fees than they would have had they shipped in fully laden. The Ginkgo and red maple trees that grew like mad in the community all came from the Orient, he told her. They weren't indigenous. They'd arrived as saplings, even as seedlings; gifts for wives and families. Some were a hundred and thirty years old. As were some of the large old houses on the other side of town—built by smugglers and stolen goods fences, low-life pirates whose descendants had become millionaires, stayed long enough to have streets named after them, then moved away.

He pronounced the meal a complete success—and she thought so too.

The warm night rustled indoors, touching his fine curly hair, making it glitter a strand at a time in the candlelight. His eyes were huge and dark and compelling.

He hadn't said anything about how she looked, so she decided to bring it up in a roundabout way, by telling him that if she'd invited Bill Tierney instead of him, Bill would have dressed all wrong for the occasion.

Jonathan almost frowned; then, casually, with the wineglass tipped up to his mouth, in preparation for a sip, he said:

"One of the few advantages of aging is that generally the older one gets, the easier it is to figure out what to wear."

"You make yourself seem as though you're a hundred years old!" she protested.

"I recently read that people's height begins to decline after the age of thirty-five. That means I've already begun to shrink. Horrible, huh?"

Unwilling to allow him to belittle himself, she said, "I think you're beautiful."

There was an embarrassed momentary silence.

"Thanks," he said. "I wasn't fishing for a compliment."

"*I* was." She stood up, taking the dishes.

"Didn't I say how marvelous you looked?"

"No."

"Well, I thought it."

"I can't read your thoughts," she said. "Coffee?"

When she returned to pour it, he was standing out on the deck.

"You aren't angry at me, are you?" he asked.

"No-o. Of course not."

"It's really a great night," he said, more softly. "It hasn't been a terrific summer for weather. Too much rain. It was cool most of July. We used blankets at night, as late as the first week of August. Damp, muggy, misty: weeks at a time. But it's going to be really fine from now on. Better than all the rest of the summer."

Odd; Stevie had thought exactly that this evening, watching the sunset, the geese flying.

"If it doesn't storm again," she said.

"It won't." He replied so firmly, she asked how he could be certain. She wished she could see his eyes as they spoke. How could she steer him back inside where they could look at each other? So much seemed to depend on that.

"I'm used to feeling out the moods of places I know," he said. "It's a telluric connection; as though a plumb line were dropped down from inside me, right into the center of the earth, with everything— the weather, the life placed around us—in a certain relationship. I don't feel this everywhere, of course. Not in the city, for example. Here at Sea Mist, I do."

He was the one who turned and led her inside then, where she refilled their coffee cups. Facing him over the flicker of candlelight, Stevie felt better; he'd seemed so distant out there for a minute.

"You know something," he offered, apropos of nothing in particular, "you remind me of another girl, a girl named Fiammetta, in a story I'm working on."

"A new show?"

He seemed surprised at her question. "Yes. A new one."

"I loved *Little Rock.* I saw it twice. Downtown, and when it moved to Broadway." She almost immediately regretted her gushing. The last thing she wanted was for him to think her a groupie. "Everyone is recording 'Unreal,' you know," she added, hoping to make good her error.

"Not everyone," he said, barely holding back a smile.

"Everyone is. Come on. It's all right to be proud about that."

"Billie Holiday isn't recording it."

"She's dead. Even I know that."

"Just testing."

"Who's Fiammetta?" she asked. She was dying to know whom or what he thought could compare to her.

"A young lady in thirteenth-century Florence, whose favorite hunting falcon has flown off. She sends three suitors to find a new one for her, equal to the first in speed, beauty, and prowess. Every time they return with a great hunting bird, she criticizes their selections. Each time she describes her falcon to them, it's different: more fabulous than before. Each suitor goes farther and farther away from her, for longer periods of time, searching for a falcon she will accept. When they return, Fiammetta's idea of the falcon has become more exaggerated. Two suitors give up eventually. But one, Gentile, continues to search. You see, he's come to think of Fiammetta herself as so extraordinary, so unobtainable, that he believes no bird he will ever encounter can come up to her—to his own—expectations."

Stevie would have to ponder that fable later on, she thought. Meanwhile, she had a question: "Does he marry her at the end, anyway?"

"See the show."

"How can I, if it isn't even completed yet?" Then, "Do you think I'm like that? Chasing after rainbows? Is that why you told me her story?"

"No. Chasing after ideals, perhaps. But don't stop."

"And you?" She meant to ask if he were that ideal, and unobtainable.

"Oh, naturally, I'm still going after a few ideals too, although I ought to know better by now. Otherwise I'd stop writing music, stop writing shows. I'd give up looking for the perfectly appropriate melody, the most wonderful new modulation, the ideal form for a song."

She wondered if what he was saying explained why he always seemed to be looking just to one side of her, or any object he observed: as though he were looking for the music inside it. It was thrilling to think that besides being so handsome, so desirable, he was also an artist. Would he one day write something for her? A song? A show?

So she led them into a conversation about theater and the music world he moved in—the people, the names, the entrepreneurs, directors, writers. Jonathan smiled indulgently as though he'd been waiting for this, but he did allow himself to talk about it. Doing so, he revealed another side of his personality; he was sincere and comic at the same time, blasé but intensely opinionated, yet never critical of anyone. His main targets of abuse seemed to be the various systems he'd gotten involved with—publishing houses, recording labels, conglomerate producers. He told her that he preferred live cabaret performances of his songs best of all—or intimate stage productions in small theaters. It was all getting out of hand now, his career expanding too quickly, onto Broadway stages and who knew, films too. Of course, he understood that was a natural progression, given the need for good material in all media. And he did like the challenge of a big stage, a large orchestra and cast. So long as he could still return to his origins, to small theaters, whenever he wanted to.

He said he was merely being realistic. But Stevie thought he was finer than that—in touch with himself and his wants and needs, overmodest, mature, filled with integrity.

Then he looked at his watch and said it was time for him to go.

It was barely eleven o'clock.

"I still have work to catch up on," he apologized. "Thanks for a lovely dinner."

She'd somehow expected he would stay longer, make it easier for her. What could she do all night by herself, after all this stimulation? She'd go mad.

"Come by for that bookshelf checking," he reminded her.

She almost said yes, she would, right now. But he had work to do. She mustn't get in the way of his composing. That would be the worst thing she could do.

"Tomorrow afternoon?" she asked.

"Anytime."

"Good night," she said, brightened by this.

And was rewarded. He said good night, and quickly leaned forward to kiss her cheek. She sensed it coming and turned her head, taking the kiss on her lips, as one of his hands touched her left ear with the merest brush of a finger. A softness of lips, a tiny caress, and nearness. Then he was gone.

CHAPTER NINE

The phone was ringing again: for the third time that morning. How was he going to get any work done? He'd been at the piano all morning, trying to work out the big chorus, a triple madrigal, that would be sung when all three of Fiammetta's suitors began their first journey in search of the falcon. But he just couldn't get past one point in the piece; he didn't know why. Barry's lyrics were fine—the interweaving seemed right—why then couldn't he make it come out sounding medieval? It always ended up vaguely French, vaguely like Gounod. He could already picture the looks on Saul's and Amadea's faces when he played the chorus for them; she would be kind, but afterward Amadea would sweetly ask him to look it over again. Saul would run his big fingers through his thinning long hair, and drop his head, unable to say anything, but secretly fuming, or despairing that he'd ever allowed the others to talk him into anything as monstrous as a medieval musical. Maybe Jonathan ought to set this chorus aside altogether. Come back to it when the rest of the score was done.

And the phone didn't stop. He'd had to take the first two calls this morning. Daniel, reporting in at 9:00 a.m. It was teatime in London, and Dan was off to tea with Lord and Lady Someone-or-other, connected with the network. Then he would be off to dinner with Ricky and Andre who'd moved to England a year ago. Then off, afterward, to bars. "The sleazy ones," Dan hoped, "in South London. With motorcycle boys." What had Jonathan been up to? Dan managed to ask in the last moments of their ten-minute transatlantic call. "Nothing. Composing. I had dinner with the Locke girl last night. Lady Bracknell's ward. Over at her house. She was alone too." Dan had replied, "You poor dear! You are having it bad there, aren't you? Why not close up the house and go back to the city?" "Because I'm working," Jonathan had said. Then the international operator interrupted, and it was love and kisses, good-bye, ta!

Working. Trying to work. He'd been stuck since the night of the storm, if he really admitted it. Yesterday was almost a total loss. He'd awakened late, found he couldn't concentrate at all, went for a walk on the beach, sat down with Stevie on her blanket, then—after she'd left the beach—had tried to work later on, but again couldn't concentrate. Thus the recourse to the piano. He'd spent most of last night playing out the score up to this point. That hadn't been wasteful. He'd found some nice new figurations for Fiammetta's first song, incorporating his ideas of temperament à la Stevie Locke. He'd played a bit more with Gentile's prayer. That was now done, quite moving, he thought. Why was this damn chorus holding him up?

The phone rang and rang. Then stopped.

The second phone call of the day had been from his long-time collaborator Barry Meade. Business, Barry reported. Jonathan knew better. It was check-up time. Barry was getting worried. He'd been worried right from the beginning on *Lady and the Falcon*: anxious from their first meeting over the scenario. Jonathan understood why. Successful as *Little Rock* had been, Barry felt this was the show that would make him or break him. He'd never really wanted to write musicals in the first place. Barry was a poet. He was uncomfortable among show people: uncomfortable to the point of distress around anyone, it seemed, except Amadea and Saul, Daniel and Jonathan, and a few others. He belonged in some small upstate New York college, teaching English literature and writing his lovely poetry. Not out here in the public eye, writing the book and lyrics to all-star, million-dollar musicals for Broadway. Implicit in every question he asked Jonathan, every discussion they had about the punctuation of a lyric he'd written for *Lady and the Falcon*, was Barry's real question—had he overreached himself, was he deluding himself;

off-off-Broadway shows were one thing; was he good enough to be writing something this big, this important? Jonathan felt like a convent mother with him, at times; spiritual and rational support was endlessly needed. And what if the show *did* fail? Jonathan would always have several good songs. Amadea and Saul would feel bad for a while, then, like all producers, get in line for another project. But Barry would suffer, possibly talk himself into a nervous breakdown. The responsibilities in such an undertaking seemed awesome to Jonathan. No only did he have to score a three-hour show, he had to protect the future of another man, a grown man.

Luckily, Barry had been able to keep his anxieties to a minimum in this phone call. Contracts for the British production of *Little Rock* had gone through, he said, pleased. Big bucks. It seemed the English had always had a softness for country rock music. The show would be done in the West End and the investors there were extremely enthusiastic about it. On the other hand, Barry said, progress on the film version here was still inching along at a snail's pace. There had been a nine-way conference call on two coasts yesterday: he and Amadea and Saul, their agents and lawyer; the producer in Hollywood, his choice of actor, his agent, and all their lawyers. It had gotten so confusing, Barry hadn't known who was saying what, and had demanded that every speaker identify himself before having his say. It had turned into an insane free-for-all anyway.

Hearing Barry talk business amused Jonathan. It also made him feel more at ease. He reported good work on the score. He explained the various changes in the pieces he'd been working on. Barry seemed delighted that his comic foil to Fiammetta—Giustina's— first act song would be a lullaby. "I never thought of it that way," he admitted, "but I think it's terrific." When Jonathan began talking about his modifications of Fiammetta's number, he had to explain that he thought she ought to be played by as young a performer as possible—given the enormous focus she would provide: no more than eighteen years old. Barry agreed with that too. "Marge will bitch and whine about my having to audition all those nubile young girls," Barry said. "It's my weakness, you know." Jonathan hadn't really known. Was that why Barry's wife had been so strongly supportive of his leaving Swarthmore and writing musicals with Jonathan? To keep him away from the co-eds?

To which Jonathan had said, "You ought to be out here, then. There's one perfectly nubile maiden, all of eighteen years old, alone, just waiting for her castle to be breached." He'd been teasing, of course, but when Barry dropped his voice to a baritone Jonathan had never heard before and began to ask questions, he became embarrassed at how specific the details soon became in his collaborator's imagination. "I sure wish I were there," Barry said, concluding, realizing that Jonathan's answers were getting more and more vague. Jonathan was sorry he'd brought up Stevie at all, glad he hadn't been stupid enough to say anything about her serving breakfast coffee to him, naked in bed, yesterday morning. Barry might have really gotten ideas and on some pretext of the score, flown out to Sea Mist.

The phone started ringing again. Damn! He ought to have taken it off the receiver.

"Hello!" he finally said, hoping he sounded evil.

"I thought you were out," a woman's voice replied. It took Jonathan a minute to recognize the voice as that of Janet Halpirn, Dan's ex-wife.

"Sorry, Jan. I was pretending it was off the hook."

"I'm glad you stopped pretending. Is Dan there?"

"London. For a month. I'll give you his phone number there."

"London!"

"He gets all the breaks," Jonathan commiserated.

"That's awful! He was supposed to take the boys this weekend. We planned it a month ago. Christ! Pete's going to hit the roof. Didn't Dan even mention it to you before he left?"

"You know how scatty Dan gets when he's traveling. I have to make sure he's packed underwear and socks."

"I know."

Here they were: two wives talking about the same husband, comparing notes. He liked Janet, however, which made it less banal. And he hated defending Dan to her.

"I talked to Dan this morning, and he didn't mention it then either," Jonathan said. "I'll bet he was afraid to say anything."

"Knowing Dan's great love of avoiding scenes unless he has the starring role, I'd have to agree," she said. "Well, I guess Pete will simply have to swallow his disappointment."

"I'll take the kids," he offered. He liked Dan's and Janet's boys, Ken, eleven, and Artie, nine. They'd spent a month out here, July, in Sea Mist, already; been out various times on weekends earlier that year and during previous seasons.

"Not if you're too busy to answer the telephone, Jonathan. I couldn't. They'd drive you nuts."

"So? I'll be a little busier. Put them on the seaplane after school. I'll meet them at the dock."

"I can't," she wavered.

"I'll be done with my work today by the time they arrive."

"They do like you," she said. "Of course they'll miss not seeing Dan."

"He'll call in the morning. He calls every day."

"Really?" Surprise and irritation. "He never used to call me regularly when he was away." Then, the old Janet, more relaxed. "I suppose that's why you two are still together after eight years. We didn't last half that long." A pause, then, "On the seaplane? Are you sure? They're only kids."

"They've been on it before. We always take it," Jonathan insisted. "Otherwise it takes all evening to get here. Believe me, Jan, bicycle riding is more dangerous. Book them for a four o'clock flight."

The idea grew more attractive to him as he argued for it. He hadn't been alone with the boys in almost a year. It would give him a chance to relate with them without the ever-present Daddy of Daniel hanging over them. They were good children—Ken a little moody, preternaturally intelligent; Artie playing on his younger status, seeking attention and affection, but funny and charming too.

"You are patient," she said, "to put up with all of us, and our mix-ups. Maybe that's the secret of loving Daniel."

"The secret of loving Daniel is to ignore him completely half the time, which he will resent, and to give him all your attention the other half, which he'll also resent. Confused, ambiguous, he'll eventually surrender. For example, when he calls tomorrow, I'll act as though we'd already discussed the boys' visit, and it's nothing out of the ordinary. He'll be surprised, apologetic, then more than a little annoyed by my tactic. All of which will satisfy me. End of incident."

"Virtue triumphant," Janet said, laughing. "You really do have him psyched out, don't you?"

"We're absolutely alike," Jonathan said. "So it's easy. The only difference between us is that he does it openly, loudly, dramatically. Whereas I do it quietly, covertly, more subtly. How's Pete?" he asked, curious about the younger man Janet had been living with for the last year or so.

"He's fine. Got a new motorcycle. A big old thing from the fifties. Called an Eagle. Makes more noise than a Boeing 747 taking off. We ride around on it all the time. I feel the way I always thought I would when I was a teenager and used to see boys on motorcycles speeding by."

"How?"

"Like a slut!" She laughed, then said more seriously, "Pete and Ken are on the outs again. If Ken says anything to you…"

"If he does, I'll listen, discuss it; but I won't snitch on him."

"It's not snitching! I'm his mother."

"Ken will think of it as snitching."

"Spoilsport! Here's some background if he does say anything. Ken told Pete he was overcompensating for a real fear of lack of masculinity by doing all these dangerous sports—you know, the motorcycle, the hang gliding, the bobsledding. Pete got huffy and suggested he become gay like Ken's father. Ken hit him, and said he was proud of his father, gay or not. You know they marched together in the Gay Pride Parade last year."

"Gay Daddies. I know. I marched too."

"Well, I made Ken apologize to Pete; but they haven't spoken in the two days since. Pete says Ken has a lot of unresolved feelings about growing up with a male gender identity. He blames Dan for that. Blames me too."

Jonathan began to get angry. "Ken's only eleven years old, for chrissakes. Why should he have any feelings about gender? He probably hasn't even had an erection yet."

"Don't yell at me. I don't want to be referee."

"But if Pete's pressuring him, making him play baseball and all that…"

"Ken would rather be tortured to death than play baseball. Come on, Jonathan. Don't you start with stereotypes. Pete isn't a father. He just wants to be liked by the boys."

"If they're hitting each other…"

"Pete's not *hitting* my children. He'd be out on his ass tomorrow. Only *I'm* allowed to strike my children in this house." She sighed. "And God knows, sometimes I wish I could bring myself to do it."

"All right," Jonathan said, calming a bit. "Maybe some time out here is exactly what the boys need."

"It's what *I* need! Jonathan, don't rile them up against Pete, please?"

As he didn't say anything, she asked again.

"Well, I love them," Jonathan began, "and I don't want to see them growing up with all the sexist shit I had to put up with."

"And I love all of you, remember," she said wearily. "Seaplane at four?"

"At four," he agreed. "You have the phone number for the reservations?"

"Somewhere. You're sure about this?"

"Ask the kids. They may not want to come with Dan away."

"Of course they'll say yes. They're crazy about you."

"Which can't please Pete too much."

"They're lucky kids, having three fathers, I tell them." That felt good hearing too. It would be fun here with Artie and Ken; and it would give him a chance to try to undo some of Pete's uptightness.

"Seaplane at four!" he said.

"I hope you won't be sorry," she said before hanging up.

CHAPTER TEN

Jonathan hadn't been out of his house all morning. Stevie wondered if he was ill—or merely hard at work. She'd restrained herself from taking him up on his invitation to check his library all day yesterday: restraint that had somehow pleased her, filled her with an air of expectation and a feeling that if she could only be patient, she would be rewarded as she had been with his kiss.

Seeing him step onto his deck shattered that resolve. She wanted to do something to get his attention: call to him, wave, do something to make him notice her. Perhaps he was merely taking a break from his composing, a breather? Either that, or he was still composing in his mind, away from his desk, or his piano, before going back inside to write it down. Hadn't other composers worked that way? Hadn't Mozart composed entire overtures in his head during stagecoach rides to the cities where the operas were to be premiered? She couldn't disturb him now, not with that possibility. Although she couldn't think of a better time, either.

Jonathan stepped inside again, and Stevie leaned back in her chaise longue and looked up. Another splendid, sunny, hot day. Really beautiful. Jonathan had been right about that too. There didn't appear to be a hint of a cloud. How long could it last?

He was outside again. In addition to his faded forest green gym shorts, he had thrown a pale blue and white checkered shirt over his shoulders, without buttoning it. Its short sleeves were rolled up almost to his shoulders. He swept a pair of sunglasses off the deck table, and walked out to the beach.

She stood up, and waved, but didn't call out to him. He evidently didn't see her, but headed away, to the surf.

She didn't know what to do. She couldn't let another day pass without at least saying hello to him. Not after that night.

She pulled on her shorts over her bikini, tied a kerchief around her head, and followed him onto the beach.

He was far ahead, ankle-deep in the surf, looking out to sea, then walking with his head down again. He might still be composing in his head.

Feeling foolish, Stevie dawdled farther and farther behind, thinking she might just sit down somewhere, look at the ocean, and wait until he passed her on his way back to the house.

She'd just settled herself on a dry-looking sand cliff, cut out of the beach by the tide, when she saw him leave the water's edge and trudge up to a wooden stairway that she knew led to the harbor area and little village.

She would follow. Meeting there would seem even more natural than on the beach, far more coincidental.

As she came out of the surrounding foliage onto the harbor, she saw that he had walked past the village, around the rim of the harbor and onto a jutting pier, where he sat down and lighted up a cigarette.

It was late afternoon, on a Friday, yet the place seemed as quiet as it had all week. Only a few yachts remained bobbing slightly at tether in the little harbor, two lovely sleek sailboats, their sails gathered up around their masts like bundles of laundry, and a few smaller boats. In July, Stevie knew the harbor was noisy and crowded, filled with boats and people. Now the only activity was on a flatbed barge for shipping large deliveries that was moored to one side; the two workers on it sat out of the sun under a striped, faded awning, drinking beer, their feet straight out, their big, brown boots making them look like clumsy giants, awkward and out of place in this resort of bare feet and fragile summer shoes.

The rest of the harbor village seemed equally still. The two stores for food and liquor were open. The grocery store looked empty. Stevie could see the checkout girl through the plate glass window, reading a magazine on the counter. In front of the liquor store, the owner's wife was sitting out on a little deck, tanning, her sunglasses pushed off her wide, red face, her feet straight out, as though she'd been immobilized by the heat. The two little restaurants hadn't yet opened for the weekend. Stevie supposed they would wait until just before dinnertime. The boutique where she'd bought her slacks and blouse was closed, however: its sale sign removed, its shades down and windows shuttered as though for a hurricane. A handwritten sign tacked onto one shutter thanked its customers and gave the date next spring when the store would reopen.

Stevie decided she might go pick up a few more groceries, then wander out to the pier where Jonathan sat. Or she would…

The telephone booth at the harbor attracted her eye. It sat right there in the middle of the dock, near the ferry loading area. She suddenly felt an awful need to talk to someone.

"Please charge this to my home number," she said to the local operator and waited. It was Friday, after four o'clock in the afternoon. Would Rose Heywood have already left? Or would she still be on campus? It was the first weekend of the semester. A glorious one.

"Hello!" she said. She'd gotten the faculty office building operator and asked for Rose.

"So do whatever you think best," Stevie heard Rose Heywood saying. Then, in a different, impatient, more official voice into the receiver, "Yes? What is it?"

"It's Stevie," she said, feeling as though she had interrupted Rose in something important. "Stevie Locke."

"Is that you, Stevie? Wherever are you?"

"Not at school."

"I know that, dear. Wait a minute, Stevie." She half covered the receiver and could be heard talking to someone else. Back again. "How tiresome some of these girls are. As for you, dear, I'm devastated. Where on earth are you?"

"Sea Mist."

"Where?"

"On eastern Long Island. At my parents' summer house. I'm here all alone. Thinking."

"Oh, dear!"

Stevie had to laugh. Just hearing Rose made her feel better, less lonely.

"Are you ever coming back to us?"

"That's just it; I don't know."

"Take the semester off, then," Rose said. "Take your lovely boyfriend and go skiing in the Alps or off on an ocean cruise."

"I'm thinking about him too," Stevie said.

"I see!"

She didn't know how much she could tell Rose. She used to tell her everything last year. But then last year there wasn't that much to tell, was there?

"Rose, I'm in love. Or infatuated. Or something. With someone else. His name is Jonathan Lash. He's a composer."

"You little beast. You ought to have told me that right away, instead of all this shilly-shallying about thinking. Is he handsome?"

"He's scrumptious," Stevie said, relaxed, and realizing that of course she could tell Rose everything. Rose was...well, she was Rose, wasn't she?

She began a description of Jonathan that soon had Rose cooing on the other end. When she mentioned the extreme whiteness of his groin against the caramel color everywhere else, Rose interrupted.

"How much of him have you seen?"

"All. One morning."

"One morning, yet!" Rose mocked. Then, "Well, it sounds too wonderful for words. And I don't blame you a bit for not coming back to stupid old Smith, with an Adonis like that naked around you. In fact I'm quite envious and disturbed that you called. I'm surrounded by work and schedules, while you're off being some maiden in a bagnio."

"Hardly. Rose..." Stevie was aware her voice had expressed the uncertainty she really felt.

"What's the problem with him, dear?"

"No problem."

"There's always a problem in love, Stevie; otherwise it would soon become boring. What's yours? Is he a quadriplegic amputee?"

"No! Aren't you awful. You are jealous."

"I admitted it. Come on, puss. What is it? If the sex is terrific, it can't matter that much."

"Well…we haven't actually made love yet," she said, wondering how that would sound.

"Playing coy, aren't you?"

"Sort of. He's older than I," Stevie blurted out. "About twice my age."

"Heavens! Perhaps he can't make love after all! Darling, believe me, mid-thirties is hardly the age for geriatric impotence."

"His age is fine. I'm certain that's part of his attractiveness to me. The way he's aged, matured. It seems so…well, so authentic."

"Well, then? Don't tell me he's married. That's it! He's married. Leading you on?"

"Not really. Sort of. His lover is in London."

"Does she know about you?"

"I don't think so. Not yet, at least," Stevie hedged, then finally let it out: "Rose, his lover is a he, not a she."

Silence on the other end, then: "You are in a fix, aren't you?"

"Do you really think so, Rose?"

"Well, darling, there might be extenuating circumstances you haven't told me yet."

"Realistically, Rose!" Stevie was firm now. "No bullshit or anything."

"All right, Stevie, no bullshit. You might make love together. You might make love a dozen times, a thousand times. You might live together for years, have children and all. And I would still tell you to get away from there and come back to school. We could rig up some sort of excuse for illness for the first week of term."

"That bad, huh?"

"Are there extenuating circumstances?" Rose asked.

"Of course there are. He's alone out here. And I'm in love with him."

"Darling, it would be easy for you to be excused. I'll bear witness for your being ill."

"I'm really deranged, then?"

"You don't sound bad. It sounds quite pleasant, in fact." Rose tempered her previous words.

"I'm not coming back. I'm going to keep on seeing him."

"Despite what I said?"

"Despite it!"

"Well! Good for you, Stevie. Don't let me stop you. I'm all in favor. I've always been like the Red Queen anyway, as you know. I like to think of three impossible things before breakfast every day. Have fun. Don't suffer. Unless, of course," she added quickly, "you want to. Then luxuriate in it."

"Did you ever have an affair with a gay man?"

"Yes. But it was a bit easier then. He didn't know he was. Only found out later."

"Jonathan and Dan have been lovers since before we took the summer house. But it's not impossible, is it? Admit that, Rose?"

"Darling, if I were eighteen and footloose and attractive as you are, I'd certainly give it a try."

"Really? No bullshit."

"Really."

That seemed like the true, honest Rose Heywood. So Stevie decided to change the subject. "Will you come to see me in Manhattan some weekend?"

"Of course I will. I will miss driving down there with you, though. The new crop of girls here seems more naïve than ever before. They must be recruited from remote places in hidden away valleys on the wrong side of large mountains. And your class, well, I gave them up en masse last year. Except for you, of course."

"And look at me."

"Don't be too harsh on yourself. If you're even considering having an affair with a beautiful, already married homosexual male twice your age, I'd say you're miles ahead of these poor chickadees at school. Maybe you oughtn't to come back, after all. Perhaps you ought to get a job or something. Try the real world for a while."

"That's exactly what I was thinking. But doing what?"

"I don't know. Why not make up a list. Make up three lists. One of what you'd most like to do. Another for what you'd settle for, if you can't do the first. And a third of what you'll probably end up with, without a college diploma."

A seaplane buzzed overhead. When Stevie turned her head to watch it, it curved in a wide arc, descending into the Great South Bay, preparing to land. She could just make out Jonathan's distant figure, standing up and waving to someone inside. Then he walked over to where its passengers would disembark.

Damn. It looked like he had company. She ought to have stopped him on the beach.

"Will you make those lists, Stevie?"

"I will, Rose. I think it's a terrific idea. Will you call me when you're planning to come to the city?"

"Not for a few weeks."

"We'll lunch at Schrafft's," Stevie said. "We'll both wear little hats with veils, and eat cucumber sandwiches."

"If we can still find a Schrafft's," Rose said. "They're probably all Taco Ricos by now. Stevie?"

"Yes."

"Promise me you'll do something foolish."

"Thanks for being no bullshit, Rose. I promise." She'd barely hung up the phone when Stevie spotted Jonathan coming toward her alongside the harbor's edge. On either side of him were two little boys with flight bags slung over their shoulders. They each held one of his hands, and were talking animatedly. Jonathan had taken off his shirt, and it was pushed through the strap of another, larger canvas bag he carried over his shoulder. As they approached, she saw him in a new light—as a possible husband and father—a role unthinkable until that moment. She got shivers up her spine at the thought. All three of them stopped and turned slightly away from her. One little boy pointed to the seaplane, taking off now, gliding away on the water. Jonathan's profile was lovely; the way his chest sloped and drew in and sloped again drew her eyes; his thighs in their worn shorts; his beard curling in the sunlight. And he could be a husband and a father!

They turned, and saw her.

"Hi!" she said, a picture of spontaneity.

"Hey! Look who's here," Jonathan said, and smiled. He was clearly pleased to see her. "Stevie Locke. These are two of my best friends. Artie. And Ken."

The children wore short pants, sandals, and T-shirts with comic book characters stenciled on them. They didn't look like Jonathan: neither did they really look alike. They shook hands with her politely, however, looked at her with that typically childlike mixture of curiosity and disdain, then moved slowly away.

"Shopping?" Jonathan asked.

"On the phone. The one at the house is already shut off for the winter."

"You could use ours."

"Thanks. I wasn't thinking."

"And you still haven't come to check our bookshelves."

"I was going to. Mind if I walk along with you?"

The boys had already moved on along the boardwalk, and were talking to the sheepdog with the red handkerchief tied around its neck that Stevie had seen waiting at the dock the day of her arrival. When the dog bored them, they began a walking race along the main boardwalk, using a certain yellow fireplug they'd spotted ahead as their destination. Evidently they knew the direction of his house.

"The offer is still open," Jonathan said. Then, "Thanks for dinner. You're a good cook."

He looked rested, content.

"They're Dan's boys," he explained to her. She ought to have known. She remembered her mother and father talking about the children visiting the summer house. Lord Bracknell thought it a scandal, of course: having impressionable youths around such flaunting inverts; who knew what they might turn out to be? For once, Stevie's mother had disagreed. And Stevie herself had jumped into the argument, making certain her father knew she thought he was living in the twelfth century so far as manners and morals were concerned. It had been a delightful argument, she recalled. At the end of it, he'd gone off to his workshop muttering, and she to her bedroom, humming a tune, feeling a bit like Margaret Mead and Joan of Arc combined. Now, however, the boys' presence at Jonathan's beach house disturbed her. She knew their presence meant that he would be giving all his attention to them; and not to her. But it signified something set and settled about his relationship to Dan that made her own vague plans for herself and Jonathan more difficult to contemplate. She hid her thoughts, however, as they walked.

"They're real beach babies," Jonathan said. "Can't keep them away from here. They stayed all July."

"If you need any help with them…" she offered lamely.

"No problem at all. I sort of like having them here. We do things I wouldn't ordinarily do. We have cookouts on the barbecue. Have scavenger hunts along the beach. They're no trouble at all. And"—he smiled—"they're asleep by ten."

She wondered if that was a hint to her that he would have time to see her at night. She had to be careful she wasn't deluding herself about his interest in her because of her own intense desire for him; but it would be equally foolish to let such hints slide away without noting them.

"Hey! Look, Jonathan!" the smaller of the boys called out, pointing up to the telephone wires, where two doves were sitting next to each other. "What are they?"

"House doves," Jonathan said.

"Love birds!" the boy said. "Ick!"

"Ick!" Stevie repeated, and Jonathan laughed.

Somehow that seemed the signal for her to leave them. She would go to the beach, off this other path, get away now while she could still restrain herself from looking stupidly at Jonathan's face like a love-stricken creature herself.

Strangely, the boys both said good-bye to her. She'd assumed they'd forgotten about her. What polite, well-brought-up boys, she thought. A good point for her to use should the lovers and their children ever come up again in an argument with her father.

Later that evening, she saw Jonathan and the boys out on the oceanside deck barbecuing hamburgers and frankfurters. The boys were very active: all over the deck, doing a multitude of chores. They seemed very at home at the house, and that dispirited her, making her feel even more like an outcast there and in Jonathan's life. He waved to her, however, at one point, and invited her over to join them. Much as she wanted to, she shook her head no. Perhaps she'd go over later on, when the boys were sleeping.

After her own thrown-together dinner, Stevie sat down to make those lists Rose Heywood had persuaded her to try. The idea of not going back to school, but instead finding work, was both inspiring and disconcerting with all its possibilities. Carefully, rigorously—for this would count, wouldn't it?—she drew up three lists. Oddly, she discovered she'd like to do many things in life. She would like to be the administrator of a large company—say a fashion or interior design firm; she'd like to be a lawyer, an airplane pilot, a literary agent, a diplomat appointed to a foreign nation. Just picturing herself in the roles and regalia of such glamorous professions helped her to become interested in the list-making. She also made a fourth list, which she titled "What I could not ever endure." Heading that page was "a housewife, like my sister Liz." But the list went on to include nursing and social work. On the other hand, lay psychotherapy seemed to be exempt from this list, and indeed was placed on each of the three other ones, and finally surrounded with a penciled box on list number one. She finally put it first on her most glamorous list, even though she knew she would still have to return to school for it.

Such taking stock of her life and desires—with the aid of a brandy and tonic like the ones Jonathan had made—exhausted her. She had one moment when she thought, yes, he was inviting me, and she thought she'd go visit him. But when she stepped out onto the deck, she heard the sound of his piano, muffled and wandering, and she supposed he was working. So she went to bed instead.

She continued to procrastinate the next day too, until almost sunset. She'd seen Jonathan out on the beach with the boys part of the morning and almost all afternoon. They seemed to be so much a unit, and to be having such a good time together, she'd deliberately stayed away from them, not going out onto the sand until they'd returned home.

However, and quite terribly for her, in the light of day, the four lists she'd written up the night before seemed ridiculous. She wondered if Rose had been making fun of her in suggesting them. They now looked utterly juvenile and completely, depressingly impossible. Except of course, list four: the unendurable. At sunset, when she couldn't stand looking at them, or being by herself another moment, she left the deck chair, went indoors, showered, changed into a blouse and slacks, and strolled over to the lovers' house.

The big living area was empty, although all the glass doors were open. So, after a fast glance down the hallway toward the bedrooms, she found the library bookshelves, and began to inspect them, telling herself Jonathan and the boys had gone to the village, and would be back soon.

Within minutes, she almost forgot about them. Their library was only a single bookcase about four feet wide, that extended from the floor almost to the ceiling, but it was fascinating to her. She wasn't the kind of person who immediately turned to a bookshelf or record collection to see what kind of life or personality someone possessed; yet knowing something, even as little as she knew about Jonathan, and then looking at his bookshelves was like suddenly having a map to guide you through only vaguely apprehended terrain.

She'd expected to see books on music and the theater, so the large bottom shelf, half-filled with oversize volumes, was no surprise, richly stocked as it was. Then, too, there were several shelves of paperbacks, fiction and nonfiction, classics and popular books alike. That was also no surprise—Jonathan said both he and Dan were great readers. What stopped her, however, gave her pause, were two other sections, one of medieval and Renaissance history, and the other filled with books on astronomy and physics: titles such as *Power and Imagination in Fourteenth-Century Italy*, *The Universe: Its Beginning and End*, *Elementary Relativity*, and *The Court of Mantua*. Whose books were these: Dan's or Jonathan's? Did Jonathan's interest in the stars, which she had thought romantic and even a bit woodsmanlike on her deck that evening they'd had dinner, really signify that he had a genuine interest in and knowledge of astrophysics? That was strange in a musician, wasn't it? Or did it somehow relate to music? As in the harmony of the spheres? She'd recalled an ancient woodcut illustrating such a concept. And these books of very detailed and even pedantic historicity, did they show that he'd read a great deal before writing his show about thirteenth-century Florence? Or had he written about it because he'd read about them? What if they were Dan's books, anyway? Had his interest then become Jonathan's? How close were their interests, anyway? That might be the worst she would have to overcome: their total agreement. It would mean anything she did—even just to sleep with Jonathan once—would be perceived by them as an invasion, a sundering of their relationship.

That line of thought was far too depressing to continue. So she stood up and began inspecting the other shelves, and immediately spotted editions of a half dozen classics she'd always meant to read, books assigned to her in class that she'd never gotten around to, books that had been recommended to her, titles that had always intrigued her. She finally selected two, Balzac's *Fatal Skin*, and Virginia Woolf's *To the Lighthouse*.

That was when she heard them outside.

She looked out on the front deck, then, not finding them, walked around it to the back. No, the noises came from the ocean side. There, however, she realized why she didn't see them. They must be on the smaller private deck that opened out from Jonathan's bedroom, hidden from her by a stand of burly pines and a wooden fence. Should she call from here, or simply go in through the bedroom?

She decided on the second course. Just stepping into his bedroom and seeing the bed made her stop for a second with the memory of that morning. Then she walked to the double glass doors.

Jonathan and the two boys were at the far end of the deck, all three in the large, half-sunken hot tub built into one side of the deck, where it dropped a level to the lower terrace. He was less immersed than they, sitting on a little ledge, she supposed. He was washing the back of the smaller boy with a sponge and a bar of greenish soap. He would soap him up, sponge him off, all the while turning him this way and that, talking to the boy, then splashing water onto the sturdy little torso, then begin soaping and sponging the front of the boy. When he was done, he reached for a hose hanging on the side of the tub, and hosed off the boy to much shrieking.

"My turn," the older boy said, and went into Jonathan's arms, and allowed himself to be held and lathered up.

"What's this I hear about you and Pete fighting," she heard Jonathan say to the boy.

"Nothing."

"I don't care," Jonathan said. "Don't tell me."

"It wasn't a fight," the boy said.

"Ken hit him," the smaller boy offered. He was playing with a rubber model of what looked like a nuclear submarine.

"I apologized," Ken said quietly, pouting. "Pete's weird, you know. He's always trying something with us. Right, Artie?"

"He's okay sometimes," Artie said. He was diving the submarine in and out of the water, admiring the splashes that resulted.

"I think he has an inferiority complex," Ken said very seriously to Jonathan.

"Lift your arm," Jonathan instructed, lathering it up, then, "Why should Pete feel inferior to you? He's bigger than you. Bigger than both of you."

"I think he's afraid Mom doesn't love him as much as she does us," Ken said.

"He's jealous of Daddy too," Artie said, never stopping diving with the boat.

"Is that true?" Jonathan asked Ken.

"I don't know. Yes. I think so."

"Well, if it is true, then maybe Pete needs friends and not enemies to help him feel loved. No?"

"I love Pete," Artie said, then modified that after some thought. "Well, sometimes."

"I don't know," Ken repeated, then turned around for his back to be lathered.

"I know," Jonathan said. "I think it would be a very mature thing to do, if you talked to Pete the way you do with me and Dan."

"Maybe." Ken sounded doubtful. "You don't have to live with him, you know. That makes it different."

"Why shouldn't he feel as loved as we do?" Artie suddenly asked. "He gets to sleep with Mom. We don't."

"That's different," Ken explained. "That's sex and stuff. It doesn't always *mean* anything. Right, Jonathan?"

"Not always," Jonathan admitted.

"I think Mom loves Pete," Artie said, convincing himself. "And he does have a neat bike, too."

"That's all you ever think about," Ken said. "Pete's bike."

"It is not."

"Is too."

"Is *not!*" Artie said, and made this point by splashing water on Ken with his submarine.

Ken retaliated in kind, and soon they were shouting and splashing Jonathan, who also began shouting himself, and finally half stood up in the tub and began splashing the two of them together, with much larger waves of water. They joined sides against him, with much shouting and laughter, but soon found themselves swamped. Climbing out of the hot tub, they ran past Stevie in the bedroom doorway, into the bathroom.

"Rinse off good," he shouted after them, sitting down in the tub again. "Ken! Make sure Artie rinses. And leave some hot water for me."

He spotted her standing there.

"Hi!"

She was completely startled. She'd somehow or other felt she was invisible where she was. Now she began to blush.

"You finally came for the books," he said, sounding pleased.

She caught herself, looked down to the two paperbacks in her hand, and managed to say, "Finally. Yes." She showed him the covers and titles. He seemed to approve her choices.

"I thought no one was in the house," she explained.

"Bring me that pack of cigarettes, will you?" He pointed to a table right near her legs. She put the books down, brought the cigarettes and a lighter to him.

He opened his mouth for the cigarette, and she shook one out and placed it between his lips and lighted it. He inhaled, sighed the smoke out, and leaned back.

"That's heaven," he said.

"Tired?" she asked.

"A little. This is relaxing, though. Sit down. Go on. Pull up a chair."

She did: a little backless stool.

He smiled then, and then began to laugh—a low, quiet, private laugh.

"Look at us," he said at her puzzled look, the cigarette dangling from his lip. "Here we are again. Me naked and you dressed. It's almost becoming a habit. Like some distortion of Manet?" As she didn't get his point immediately, he said, "You know, the *Picnic on the Grass*, with the men dressed to the neck, and the naked woman."

"What would Lord Bracknell think?" she said. She realized immediately that she didn't give a damn what her father would think. Her desire for Jonathan was so intense she began to tremble. She almost reached for a cigarette herself, then remembered she hated the taste of nicotine.

"Who washes you?" she finally asked.

His eyes slid toward hers; the cigarette continued to dangle from his lips. It was getting slowly darker; the sun must have dropped below the horizon. The sky was a deep, velvety blue beyond him. She could hear the boys in the shower, laughing under the stream from the nozzle.

"Want me to play geisha for you?" she asked. She could already feel his firm flesh under her ministering hands: the soft, taut skin, the muscles, the tendons, the little places where he would be soft, at the hips perhaps, his buttocks.

As he still didn't answer, she went on to say, "I'd like to."

"Do you wash your boyfriend?" he asked in a quiet voice.

"Lean forward," she said, getting up. "I'll scrub your back for you."

As she stood and then kneeled behind him, and reached for the brush, he suddenly took her arms, and held them by the wrists. He looked at her without saying anything. It was getting darker every moment; she could barely make out his features, yet she knew where his eyes were, his mouth, his nose, almost by rote. In the bathroom, the noise of the shower went off suddenly. She could hear the boys running to another part of the house. Away from here. She almost begged him to let her. But he suddenly let go of her hands, stood up, got out of the hot tub, and strode across the deck, into the bathroom. She wondered if she should follow him, but then she heard the shower turned on again, full force, and she sat back on her heels and felt awful, bereft, humiliated, shamed, rejected.

She had to leave, right now, before he came out of the shower.

She remembered to pick up the two paperbacks, and had even partly regained her composure, when she passed the long corridor and went into the living area. The boys were at the kitchen counter bar, playing with some coloring books. They looked up as she came out.

"Hi!" they said.

"Hi!" she answered back.

"Are you staying for dinner?" Ken asked.

"No." She looked back toward the bedroom. She was certain the shower was off. She had to get out now, before Jonathan came out and saw her. "No. I just came by to borrow some books."

They seemed satisfied by that, and went back to their coloring.

She was still blushing when she reached her family's house.

"Idiot!" she said to herself. "You horny idiot. You almost ruined it!"

CHAPTER ELEVEN

Come on, lazy bones, wake up!"
Both Artie and Ken were on his bed, softly pummeling Jonathan through the sheets.

"What time is it?" Jonathan said, then managed to see the clock. "Eight o'clock. Your father won't be calling for at least another hour," he said, rolling over, and trying to avoid the boys' faces.

They settled onto the bed. Artie poked under the sheets at his chest. He rolled over the other way.

"I told you," the smaller boy concluded smugly. "Old people need their sleep more than we do."

That was all Jonathan had to hear. "All right, everyone up! Off the bed!"

In the kitchen coffee was set to brewing. It was another faultlessly clear and sunny day outside. The weather was hoiding up excellently for the boys' weekend.

They were in the kitchen too, fixing their own breakfasts with occasional comments from Jonathan, used to it by now from earlier visits to the beach house.

"Why is it you guys take so long to wake up?" Ken wanted to know.

"I can't believe you're really going to eat all that food," Jonathan said instead of answering. The boy had sat down, and placed in front of himself a container of cherry yogurt, a banana, two slices of wheat toast, a bowl of cereal with sliced fresh peaches on top, and a small dish with a rather large homemade fudge brownie. The meal was guarded on either side by tall glasses of liquids—one containing apple juice, the other milk. To Jonathan—who seldom had more than a cup of coffee before noon, no matter when he awakened—it was like facing a ten-course haute cuisine meal at Lutèce.

"Mom never wakes up easy, too," Artie said. His meal, although as large eventually as Ken's, was taken piecemeal; he'd arranged it on the kitchen counter, and would bring it to the table in stages, where he would concentrate on each item before getting up to fetch another.

"Either," Jonathan corrected.

"Mom never wakes up easy either," Artie good-naturedly repeated. Then, "That doesn't sound right."

"Well, it is," Jonathan said.

"Why?" Ken asked, barely getting the word out through a mouthful of toast.

"I don't know. Ask your English teacher."

"No. I mean, why don't you or Mom get up early?"

"He went out and partied last night," Artie said. He'd arrived at his third course: fruit.

"I was right here," Jonathan said.

He hadn't gone out last night. He'd stayed in and wrestled with that chorus at the end of the first act until he was halfway satisfied with it. In fact, he hadn't even dreamed of going out with the kids here. If Dan were home too, it would be different. Dan never gave a thought about leaving them alone while he and Jonathan went out to the little bar-disco in the village. Of course, the next question was, what would Jonathan do at the bar in the village? Stand around? Have a drink or two? Look at the dancers: younger and more attractive, gayer and more fashionable every summer? And feel older and out of place? Or was he afraid he'd bump into Stevie Locke there?

"Yeah, Jonathan, why do you sleep so much?" Artie asked.

"I guess when you're as ancient as I am, you come to realize that sleep is essentially far less threatening than being awake all the time. So, I'm naturally reluctant to leave off sleeping."

"Huh?" Artie said.

"Never mind," Jonathan said. The coffee tasted like old nailheads this morning.

"I get it," Ken said, smirking. And Jonathan indeed believed Ken did understand his point. Ken seemed to understand a great deal, whether or not he let on he did. He'd laid waste to his All-Bran, sailed into the yogurt, sipped the juice, eaten both pieces of toast, demolished the banana. He now held the fudge brownie in one hand and wielded the glass of milk in the other, taking turns with them, bite and sip.

Jonathan continued to sip at his coffee, unable to tear his eyes away from Ken's feasting, and at the same time slightly queasy about the possible consequences of such gorging.

"We saw Stevie again," Artie suddenly offered. "She's pretty!"

"She was borrowing some books," Ken explained. "While you were in the shower. That was okay, wasn't it?"

"Sure," Jonathan said. Stevie again. That had been a chancy moment at the hot tub last night. One of the closest in years. Had she seen his erection as he stood up and walked away? Probably not. Otherwise she would have followed him into the shower. Or would she have? Was she really coming on to him, anyway? Or just playing with him? Who knew?

"How come she has a boy's name?" Artie asked.

"It's short for Stephanie," Ken said. And when Jonathan wondered how he knew this, the boy asked, "Isn't it?"

"She's pretty," Artie repeated. "Prettier than Ken's girl friend."

"I don't have a girl friend," Ken said, mumbling through the brownie.

"Pete says you do," Artie countered.

"Pete's so afraid I'll grow up gay, he'll do anything and say anything to prove I'm not. Patricia is just a friend," he concluded firmly.

"But she is a girl," Artie said.

"So?"

"So, she's your girl friend."

"Phooey," Ken said. "Mom is Pete's girl friend. It's different. You have to love a girl friend. I don't love Patricia."

Jonathan marveled at how patient children could sometimes be explaining things to each other.

"But you like her, right?" Artie insisted. "Otherwise you wouldn't do things together, right?"

"Sure I like her. Her father has all these neat books on differential calculus he showed me," Ken said to Jonathan. "Filled with all sorts of shortcuts and proofs and things you can't find in regular textbooks. Patricia knows most of them already. She's showing me how to do them." His eyes almost glittered as he spoke.

"Is that true, what you said about Pete?" Jonathan asked Ken. He'd begun to feel his stomach tighten up during the conversation and it wasn't from the caffeine.

"You mean about him calling Patricia my girl friend? I guess. Who cares."

"What about what you said?" Jonathan insisted. "About Pete being afraid you'll be gay when you get older?"

"I don't know." Evasively said, head lowered, by Ken. Then, "Don't worry. I can handle Pete."

Damn it! Jonathan thought. Pete is pressuring the kid. Janet must be in on it, or at least know about it, otherwise she wouldn't have prefaced the whole thing the way she did on the telephone, or demanded to know what Ken said. Wait till Dan found out; he'd go over to Janet's and start a real scene.

"If you find you can't handle Pete," Jonathan said as emotionlessly as he could, "make certain you let me or Dan know about it. Do you hear? You don't have to take any of that reactionary crap from Pete just because he happens to be sleeping with your mother."

"I know," Ken said brightly, secretively. "I know. I marched last year. Remember?"

The boy's eyes were suddenly very grown-up. He looked and spoke to Jonathan as an equal now, not as a child. For an instant Jonathan wondered why the boy mentioned this…to help allay his fears, to say he was on their side—Jonathan and Dan's—forever? Was he…? Could he know that already? At eleven?

The phone rang, bursting in on his thoughts.

Artie was off his chair to get it in a flash, and was already accepting the call, when Jonathan arrived. Ken continued to eat, wiped his mouth, and slowly came to the phone last.

When the ten-minute operator cut in, Jonathan got on the line to have her extend the call to a half hour. She said there weren't too many Sunday calls, and she could keep this trunk line open for them.

"Hi, babe," Daniel said hesitantly to Jonathan. "How do the kids look? Okay?"

Jonathan heard a slight, unfamiliar hissing, as though another long distance line were still open: the operator's snooping in, Jonathan guessed.

"The kids look fine," he said. "But I look like hell. Damn you, Dan. I'm pregnant again."

There was an audible click. The hissing and the operator were gone. Took care of you, Jonathan thought.

"Here's Ken again," Jonathan said into the receiver. The irate operator returned to cut them off exactly at the half hour, so Jonathan couldn't say anything more than hello to Dan and then good-bye. Daniel sounded relaxed. He'd taken Jonathan's joke on the operator as forgiveness: which it wasn't. Took it rather prematurely, Jonathan thought. Took it as the easy way out for not bothering to mention the boys' visit. It annoyed him.

He sent the boys out picking beach plums, one of the few remaining bush fruits that grew at Sea Mist this late in the year. He showered and even got some exercise done in the time before they returned.

Then it was time for the beach, and another hike along the surf and into the wilder dunes distant from the community, and even inland a bit. They encountered a family of wild deer—three does, a multi-antlered buck big as a stallion, and two small fawns—who didn't seem at all shy, but merely stared at the three humans as though they were interlopers. The boys were thrilled. It was an accidental meeting, one that caused them to drop their voices to whispers. Ken and Artie talked about the deer all the way home and all through lunch.

The afternoon was spent on the bedroom deck. The boys bathed in the hot tub, while Jonathan brought out a table and chair and worked on his score. The wild deer had so excited the boys that after the bath they were unusually subdued, which suited him fine. In an hour and a half or so he managed to get a great deal of work done on the second act trio between Gentile, Farnace, and Carlo—the three suitors—and felt as though he were finally back on the road to getting the score in shape.

Ken was on the chaise longue, cream smeared over his cheeks and forehead, much reddened yesterday and today, a long yellow shirt of Dan's covering him almost down to his knees, a green plastic visor over his eyes casting a lurid and ghoulish glow on his features, a tall glass of lemonade on the side table. He was reading *Astronomy* magazine. Artie was still in his bathing suit, sitting on the deck, quietly playing with some driftwood boats Dan had made several years back, kept in the summer house. Once, when Ken looked up from his magazine, he caught Jonathan staring at him, and smiled.

"Why are you staring?" he asked.

"I'm not," Jonathan said. "I'm staring out into space, thinking. We composers do it all the time."

"He's staring because you look funny," Artie said, not even lifting his head from his playing.

"I do?" Ken said, and was amused. "How?"

"Just funny," Artie said.

"Like what?"

Like an underage Hollywood girl trying to play movie star, Jonathan thought. "Like an Egyptian," Artie said, finally looking up.

"You mean a mummy?" Ken asked.

"No. A real Egyptian. I once saw a picture of an Egyptian king at the beach," Artie explained.

"Must have been King Farouk," Jonathan said.

"Well, I don't feel like a king," Ken said, huffily. "Unless they get sunburned too."

The last seaplane back to the city was at sunset, and Jonathan managed to get the boys packed and down to the dock in time. He sat on the pier, watching the seaplane sail out into a huge, orange, gibbous sun over a glittering blue bay. A mild prevailing easterly blew at the back of his neck, and he had to lift his jacket collar, feeling his hair—too long since his last haircut—rippled by the breeze.

What kind of life was this, he wondered, with everyone he loved always going away from him, leaving him here, on this little jetty, watching them fly off?

Don't get into that, Jonathan, he warned himself. Not now. Go back and finish that chorus.

Is that why? Just to write a few songs?

As good a reason as any other. Go home. Why feel bad? The boys had been here all weekend. Dan's boys. Your boys too, by default. If only Janet would give them up to him and Dan for the next few years, until they were safely through adolescence. Her life—especially her emotional life—was far too unstable to raise children. Alan, Hugh, and now Pete: the worst. He didn't even have a job. Ran around on motorcycles, parachute jumping, drinking beer, in general acting like a seventeen-year-old himself. Was that any way to gain someone like Ken's respect? They'd be better off here, even at the apartment on Central Park West. Anything was better than being with Pete. Or would their presence drive Jonathan and Dan apart, instead of bringing them closer?

Go home. Start working.

The day was settling around him with a soft pink glow as he stood up from the dock and began walking home. For the first time so far this summer, his sockless ankles were chilled. At home, he began to shut all the glass doors, and even a few windows, and checked the fireplace. More than enough logs. He hadn't built a fire since the night of the storm. Stevie Locke. What did she want?

The cup of tea he brewed made him sleepy. Why was that? It had as much caffeine as coffee, which always woke him up. Perhaps it was associative. Whenever he was ill as a child, his mother would bring him big mugs of tea, laced with sugar and lemon, and he would soon go to sleep after drinking it. Had she laced something else into the tea? He also remembered her feeding him bowls of fluffy-looking creamed soups when he was sick: cream of mushroom, cream of celery. He wondered if he would feel sleepy if he ate a bowl of creamed soup. In some ways, childhood was better, wasn't it? All but for the utter dependence a child had, or his parents insisted he have. Jonathan had always hated and rebelled against that dependence. He tried to instill that same rebellion in Dan's boys.

He finally gave in to the drowsiness, and napped on the living room sofa. Awakened, more than two hours later, he felt out of time, off schedule, uncertain of what he really wanted to do. He turned on the radio, and quite by accident just managed to tune in the opening bars of Mozart's autumnally beautiful last Piano Concerto in F. The originality and the subtlety of the interwoven piano and orchestra impressed him as Mozart's work always did. But this time he began contemplating other, nonmusical matters: how at the time of this work, one of Mozart's last, the composer was the same age as Jonathan now, at the end of his career, with so much behind him, operas, concerti by the dozen, string quartets, piano sonatas, choral works, symphonies. Of course he'd begun earlier. But that wasn't the entire answer. Composing must have meant more to Mozart than *The Lady and the Falcon* meant to Jonathan, for him to have worked so indefatigably. Or had Mozart more energy—more will even? Was the current race of men really degenerate in the truest sense of the word?

Thinking of Mozart led him to want to listen to more of the composer's music. He found a cassette of highlights from *The Marriage of Figaro,* and listened to the by now familiar but unendingly lovely arias, trios, and duets. When he came to *"Non sono pus,"* he immediately imagined Cherubino—Mozart's mezzo-soprano as a love-struck boy—as Stevie Locke.

What was he going to do about her? It was becoming increasingly clear she was someone he would have to deal with. Already he felt some kind of tenuous presence linking her parents' house to this one—a link that had never been there before, which must mean that they had already forged some kind of relationship.

After the aria was over, he stood up, and walked to the west window and looked out. She hadn't returned to the city yet; two windows showed lights on in what he remembered to be the living room of the old, clapboard house. Hadn't she said she would only remain out here a week?

That was disturbing. Perhaps he ought not jump to any conclusions, but simply look hard at the facts of the situation. She had come out here alone, she said, to work on various crises in her young life. Understandable. Objectively speaking—and who could be more objective than Jonathan, who would soon be auditioning scores of young girls for the role of Fiammetta?—Stevie Locke was beautiful: slender, lithe, with attractive and well-sized breasts, a waist you could put two hands around easily, a scrumptious ass, long golden legs, smooth, tight skin, lips that were designed for kissing and uttering soft pleas and obscenities, and… Large, gray eyes, slightly speckled with other colors. Her brother Jerry's mischievous smile. Barry Meade would cream in his shorts just looking at Stevie. Marge would divorce Barry if she ever saw them together. That was fact number one. Objective. Indisputable.

That was fact. Now for the speculation. It seemed clear from what happened around the hot tub that Stevie Locke wanted him. Him, not her boyfriend Bill, not the two Halley boys she'd seen on the beach, in the surf. Him. But was that true? He would have to review the progress of events from the beginning to check it out. After all, it was still only speculation.

She'd arrived here at some unknown time. He'd first seen her on the beach. She'd waved and said something. Then nothing for a day and a half. The storm. She'd come in, and had tried to talk to him about her life. He hadn't allowed that, but had let her stay over when she seemed ready to go to sleep at the fireplace. So far, no problem. The next morning she'd served him coffee. Had he been more awake then he might have noticed her behaving oddly. All he saw was that she was being rather quiet. Expected. And that he'd had to pull up his sheets. Then, later that day on the beach, he'd been friendly, gone over to her blanket. *That* was when she brought up the morning. *That* was when he first began to think she was flirting. Then the dinner invitation. The dinner, all very polite and easy, with the friendly little meaningless good night kiss—a kiss he would give to anyone after a pleasant dinner unless she had third-degree burns on her face, or some signs of syphilitic degeneration. Then Dan's boys had come and they'd met her at the harbor. A nice, brief little talk before she'd turned off and gone to the beach for a swim. Why had she left so suddenly? He'd assumed they would walk home together. So had the kids; that's why they'd run ahead. Nothing for another day or so, then she arrived to borrow the books, and had wanted to wash his back in the hot tub. Another friendly gesture, no? "Who washes you?" she'd asked, probably having seen him wash Ken. Why make so much of it?

But he had. He'd heard her voice, the low, oboelike quaver in her voice, almost a catch at every other word, as she'd asked him. He'd felt that presence in the small distance between them, and it had been a palpable thing—real sexual tension. The sudden touch of her hands on him, the dry heat of her skin, the eagerness of her fingers, the overwhelming feeling that something was going to happen if he didn't get up and out of the tub immediately!

Right, Jonathan. She'd scared you. An eighteen-year-old girl had frightened big bad you with her probably unconscious desire, and slight horniness. Scared you, but turned you on too. Admit it.

What had he thought she'd do anyway, with the kids in the house, not far away, with him in the tub. Really! All she'd wanted was to wash him, as she said.

No. That wasn't true. She wanted him.

Back to the facts. Daniel was being an absolute son of a bitch. He was in London, having a ball, really on air, fucking everything that moved, being bowed and scraped to professionally, having tea with royalty and getting off all his burdens on Jonathan. Again. He'd not even asked Jonathan to go with him to England. It had been only a two-week trip at first, true. But then it had become extended in advance to three weeks, then a month, and now after only a week look at what a mess their relationship was in. Damn. That was the betrayal, not his screwing around with some Elephant and Castle bike boy.

Fact: Jonathan was horny too. Yesterday evening he hadn't even had to fantasize in order to get hard. It had just happened, like that. He hadn't had sex since Dan had gone: hadn't picked up anyone at the village bar-disco, as Dan had assumed he would, if only for hygienic purposes.

Once that fact too was admitted, Jonathan needed a drink. After a minute during which he considered alternatives—opening a book and trying to read, going back to his desk and the almost accusingly unfinished score—he sat down with the drink and went on.

Men and women had sex. It was that clear. Except, of course, when there were taboos: mothers and sons, fathers and daughters, sometimes aunts and nephews. Genetic stuff. Otherwise they had sex: period. They did so past social taboos all the time, past age differences, past color and size differences, and language barriers. None of these were any problem. Men and women had sex.

Jonathan, however, did not have sex with women—or at least hadn't in several years, and then always unexpectedly: with his roommate's sister at their shared, off-campus apartment, Ernie talking out loud in his sleep in the next room; with another girl, Yukio, on the beach one night near a campfire, among a group of other people their age, all of them off somewhere in the dunes; once too with Daniel and that black model Jonathan had always thought was a spectacularly good transvestite until that slightly druggy night.

What was that? Three times in his life? Nothing, compared to the number of men he'd bedded and been bedded by—before and even since he and Daniel began living together. And there was an essential difference in the two experiences, beyond the obvious ones. With the women, Jonathan had always been surprised by how suddenly, totally aroused he'd gotten, how passionate they'd been, and how vague, amorphous, somehow unfocused and primitive their activity had been together. He and Dan could make love for hours, playing each other's bodies like the various dials and panels of a great synthesizer, up to and away from climaxes, expertly, rhythmically. With other men, the rhythms might be different—faster, more jarring for rougher sex; or slower, more exotic, sinuous and twisting; sometimes enlivened by sudden role switches and mind games. All his times with women seemed completely mindless, unsophisticated, mere wallowings in the dark, too quickly over for experimentation, for the intensity to build to a level where he could begin to really enjoy it.

Then there were the different emotional perspectives. Jonathan had a thousand ideas about men, fantasies, images, words spoken, glances given, that combined worked on him constantly whether he was aware of them or not. He seemed to hold few emotional correlatives about women. He couldn't contemplate being hurt by a woman, for example, being in anguish over one, even a woman he might love: certainly not the way he could be distressed over something Daniel did. It wasn't the Venus and Adonis myth but that of Gilgamesh and Enkiddu—the first written love story—that appeared to guide Jonathan's fate in love. It seemed he had to battle another man: and to love him at the same time. Daniel was his eternal mystery—not Stevie Locke, or Janet Halpirn, who he believed he could usually understand as though their skulls were transparent—their thoughts written out fully in tiny neon lettering, impossible to misconstrue. Dan, even Barry Meade sometimes, would do something that would leave Jonathan in a cold sweat of misunderstanding, outraged and confused. That's what goaded him, infuriated him, fascinated him: not Amadea being Amadea.

That being so, conclusions were in order. Refill on the Dewar's, please.

Seeing Stevie would not be fulfilling because it would most likely *not* be knock-down physically orgiastic, which was what he really needed right now. For that he'd do better to take the seaplane to town tomorrow and park his act in the Tubs with the door open.

Seeing Stevie would also not be adequate compensation for what he saw more and more as Daniel's disloyalty to him; that could only occur if the emotional content of a new affair were equal in intensity—if only temporarily—to their own relationship. An affair with someone's houseboy out here, say. Some number he'd looked at guardedly all summer. If any were foolish enough to have allowed themselves to still be stuck out in Sea Mist this late.

Seeing Stevie might have other consequences. Lord and Lady Bracknell might somehow or other discover it, and pull off some tacky number—from shotgun wedding to arrest for impairing the morals of a minor: was she still a minor at eighteeen? he wondered. Then too, she could get pregnant. She must be taking the pill, no? She did have a boyfriend. A boyfriend. That was another possible consequence: what if he found out? More important—and more possible than any of these—what if Stevie really developed a passion for him. That might end up being torture.

No, it wasn't worth it. Not at all. No matter how horny he was. Too complicated, even for a flirtation. Not enough rewards in it for him. He'd go to the bar tonight or tomorrow night, and pick up someone there. Even a night passed flirting with one of the straight guys hanging around would be more satisfying. At least that would provide him with some fantasy material for when he next masturbated.

That accomplished, Jonathan finished off his drink, got up, ate a cold hamburger left in the refrigerator, looked over his score briefly, making notes about what he would be working on tomorrow, then went out onto the deck.

Stevie's house was dark now. Gone to bed already? Or had she taken the last ferry back to the mainland? Perhaps it was better this way.

It was a clear night out, clear as the previous half dozen nights. The star-filled sky seemed divided by the thick band of the Milky Way, stretching north to south. Meteors streaked toward the horizon, bursting white and green and blue. Weren't they the Perseids? A sliver of moon was descending to set. The surf softly crashed. He walked toward it, feeling the sand cool against his feet. He looked up, felt the enormous canopy of the heavens, then he relaxed, and began to hear a familiar melody inside him. Two bars, then another. It was Fiammetta's song in the first act: "Why does nobody listen, when I speak of golden falcons?" A lovely arietta, that glistened and later glowed into coloratura, before ending again as a simple, moving quatrain.

He felt as though a great weight had been lifted off him. Somewhere, across the dark expanse of ocean, Daniel was sleeping, perhaps just awakening.

CHAPTER TWELVE

The next afternoon, they were walking together barefoot along the main boardwalk leading to the village where they would buy groceries, when Stevie felt a slight snag on her foot. She looked down to see blood pumping from under a deep cut on the underpad of her big toe.

"Oh, damn," she said. Stopping, she leaned on Jonathan's shoulder and angled the foot back and up. The cut flapped closed, but blood continued to seep out, defining its extent neatly.

"Does it hurt?" he asked, holding her lightly around the waist for support.

"A little." It was beginning to throb, but she thought she could handle it.

"Hold on," he said, then, reaching into the back pocket of his shorts, he brought out a handkerchief. He leaned over her and wrapped the toe tightly in the handkerchief.

"Ouch!" she said, feeling like a sissy.

"I want to keep it from bleeding too much," he said. She leaned against his arm, and Jonathan looked around without saying a word. Then he reached around her again, and she felt herself suddenly lifted up by her bottom, and slung into his arms.

"Hey!" she said. She faced him, looking backward. "I can walk on it."

"Maybe. But you shouldn't walk on it. Not until we see how bad it is."

"Jonathan! Put me down. I feel silly."

"You're light," he said, striding ahead with her. "When I get tired, I'll make you ride piggyback."

"Where are we going?"

"You'll see."

She'd said she felt silly. The truth was she felt wonderful: as light as he said she was (though she couldn't really believe that—she weighed over a hundred pounds) and somehow privileged. She couldn't remember the last time anyone had carried her like this. She supposed the last person was her father, Lord Bracknell, putting her to bed when she was a sleepy nine-year-old. Not since then. Bill certainly hadn't ever done it. And, of course, it was somewhat bridelike too, wasn't it? Being carried across a threshold by the man you loved.

They had arrived at the harbor village. She'd assumed they'd go into one of the stores there and ask for bandages, but Jonathan continued walking on past the harbor.

Holding him around the neck she could look at him closely for once without having him look back and question her. She liked looking at his profile. She found it terribly handsome, and somewhat exotic—those almost Semitically open nostrils of his, the swirling little tempests of hair where his sideburns melded into his beard. From this angle, his eyes, too, seemed slightly different: not large and round, but almost almond-shaped, long, hooded over, like snake's eyes. She could stare at him and not wish to do anything else. Just by looking at him, she would be sent off into little mental side trips, speculating on anthropology, history, color physics, anatomy, and always be able to return to his features with fresh wonder. So this is what it means to be infatuated, she told herself. How rational and yet how completely mindless it seems.

"Got a present for you, Barbara," Jonathan said to someone.

Stevie turned her head to see they were at the little post office: a tiny shacklike edifice with a small waiting area surrounded by brass drawers occupying one wall, notices tacked onto the other. A double dutch door was ajar on top, signifying that the post office was open—it was infrequently open this late in the summer.

Hefting Stevie up, he placed her on the ledge atop the double door.

Barbara was a young mother, possibly twenty-four or twenty-five years old, whose husband, Stevie knew, was an independent contractor-builder in Sea Mist. Barbara had returned to night school college, worked here a few days a week, and took care of two small girls. Already—this early in life—Barbara's skin was sallow, her eyes sad, her brown hair without sheen or luster.

Barbara didn't say hello to Stevie, she merely lifted the wrapped-up foot, took off the bloodstained handkerchief, and inspected the toe, which had begun to ooze again.

"Anything serious?" Jonathan asked. He was behind Stevie, holding her by the shoulders.

She tried not to flinch too much, as Barbara roughly handled the cut toe.

"Doesn't look bad. Nothing major. Won't even need stitches, if you keep it closed and stay off it awhile."

Stevie couldn't help notice that the woman spoke not to her, but to Jonathan. Meanwhile, the two little girls in the back of the office—who had been quietly playing in a corner—came up and stared, one of them with a thumb stuck in her candy-smeared mouth.

"The kids are always going around and getting cuts like this," Barbara was saying, rummaging through a worn oak chest of drawers for something. She pulled out an equally ravaged-looking tin first aid kit, and began to remove various objects from it: scissors, gauze, tape, and a tiny phial of some evil-looking green solution. "Damn nails on the boardwalks." She shook the little phial, opened it, and spilled some onto a bit of wadded cotton. "This is going to hurt," she said, prying the cut open with her strong fingers, and patting it with the burning solution.

The sudden shock of pain almost made Stevie fall back off the door ledge. Jonathan held her by the back. Her head rolled back against his chest. She thought she was going to faint.

"You all right?" Jonathan asked. All the pain was worth the concern in his voice.

"I think so," she breathed out.

"Barbara?" he asked.

"She'll be all right, Mr. Lash. I couldn't put this on until it was cleaned out. Never know."

She began spraying some fine mist from a little bottle onto Stevie's foot, explaining it would help eliminate the pain. Then she carefully wrapped the toe with gauze and tape.

"There you are, young lady," she said, looking at Stevie for the first time. What kind of look was that in her eyes? Certainly not compassion, Stevie thought.

"I've got some mail for you," Barbara said to Jonathan, past Stevie again, as though she weren't there.

"Don't tell me, from Daniel?"

"A letter and four postcards. We're only open once a week this late, sorry. So it does pile up. How does Dan like London?"

"Read for yourself," Jonathan said. Then, "He's working there. How's school?"

"Lots of reading." Barbara pointed to the stack of textbooks next to a crib.

"Well. You keep at it," Jonathan said. "Walt told me how proud he was you decided to finish college."

"He needs help in his business. That's why I'm learning about it."

"You ought to take one of your books and go read it outside, in the sun," Jonathan suggested. "Get some color."

"I'm looking dowdy, huh?" the woman said without a great deal of feeling.

"A little pale," he answered gently.

The look she gave him then convinced Stevie that Barbara, too, was a little bit in love with Jonathan.

"You feeling well enough to be moved, invalid?" he asked.

She was. So he lifted her up, over the door ledge, and began carrying her again.

"Better wait here," he said, pointing to a bench, "while I get the wagon and do the grocery shopping."

"I can help," she said.

"Face facts, Stevie. You're out of action for the afternoon.

You're a total, instant invalid. Stay off your foot for a day or so. Let the wound close, okay? That way you won't need to get stitches put in it."

"All right," she said. "But I don't want to sit here." It was too close to the post office, and to Barbara, who might come outside and begin talking to her.

"I'll drop you on the bench near the harbor," he said, shifting her to his other side. "There's bound to be a bit more activity there. Who knows—maybe a ferry will come in, or a seaplane."

He placed her carefully at the harbor, and she felt comfortable. She handed him her grocery list and watched him walk the hundred yards or so to the store.

That big sheepdog with the red bandanna tied around its neck was back. It had followed them from the post office. Now it nosed around under the bench, licking her outstretched hand and even— smelling the dried blood, Stevie supposed—licking the bandage on her toe until she shooed it away. The sheepdog padded over to the little wooden barrier that closed off the landing pier and sat down, its back to her, waiting as though it were expecting someone. Its master? A new master? She knew that cats searched for and went off with new masters. Buttons, her cat in the city, had once disappeared for weeks, and when it returned she discovered it had led three lives in their backyard, sleeping with and being fed by two tenants in adjoining buildings. Nevertheless, it was sad watching this dog so expectant, so patient. Feeling remorse over sending it away, she tried to get the dog's attention by calling to it.

The sheepdog turned to look at her, it even seemed to smile the way dogs do, then turned its head away and continued waiting.

The sky over the harbor was strikingly blue, shaded darker toward the horizon, softer and brighter in the middle as though it were an enormous pale taffeta ribbon. A row of little streaks of strato-cumulus clouds in one spot looked like the runs in a nylon stocking. It would get chillier tonight, she supposed. Last night had been cooler than the night before; it was September.

Her foot still hummed with pain, and a bit of an itch. Barbara had wound the bandages so tightly. Still, it was better than having it bleeding and perhaps getting tetanus. What a stupid thing to have happened, especially now that she wanted to prove how independent she was.

"Face facts," she said, repeating Jonathan's words, "you're an instant invalid."

How chivalrous Jonathan was. How sensible too. Why did she have to be in love with him, of all people? Why now, out here, with so much in her life pending? And why did it have to be so physical? She'd had lovely relationships with boys before, without that ever coming into it; Michael in high school, Marty Strauss, several years ago.

Yet it *was* physical and to deny that was absurd. After she had left the two boys coloring in the living room, Stevie had gone home to her parents' house and had tried to read the books she'd borrowed. Of course she'd failed. All she could think of was Jonathan, in the hot tub, his eyes dark and secretive, the cigarette dangling off his lower lip. She hadn't really known what she was doing when she asked to wash him; all she knew was he was there, naked, and she had to touch him. Afterward, the Balzac thrown down on the floor of her bedroom, she'd pictured the scene differently from the way it had happened.

All was the same until he moved to take her hands, to move them away from him. At that point in her thoughts, he didn't move away at all but leaned back against the edge of the hot tub as she leaned forward and softly began to scrub his back with the sponge she'd seen him use on the children. She moved up his shoulder, over his chest, in soft, deft swirling motions, finally down to his legs. His cigarette smoke curled up into her face, sweet and pungent. She inhaled it too, felt slightly light-headed from the tobacco and nicotine. When she looked at his face, Jonathan's eyes were closed, his head thrown back. She stroked along the skin of his stretched out legs, up each one. Through the soapy water she felt his tension falling away.

"Feels good," he murmured.

Her arms were around him; she dropped the sponge in the water and was using her hands to soap and lather his chest.

"Stop," he said, moaning, "it feels too good."

She wouldn't stop, though. And when her hands moved down, they met his erection, not half-hard like before, but hard, straining through the sheath of skin. She begun to stroke it and he began to sit up.

"Look, honey," he protested.

"Sit back, relax," she said.

"You don't know what you're doing," he said, his voice thick as though his mouth were cloyed with honey.

"Yes I do," she said, and went on stroking him.

He tried to stop her once more, but she was relentless. Having him this near, this much within her grasp, she wasn't about to let go of him.

The cigarette went out then, or dropped in the water. He lay back, all resistance gone, his head rubbing from side to side softly against her breasts, as she leaned forward and worked at arousing him, using both hands now, one to stroke and one to cup and fondle his scrotum. The tip of his penis alone peeked pinkly out of the soapy water, as she lathered it.

He began to gasp, and she bent down to watch his face more closely. His mouth opened slightly, his head moved from side to side more frequently, he moaned, and finally a hoarse, half-stifled cry emerged from him, as his entire body arched up out of the water, toward her, his penis entirely out of the water, full and hard in her grip. Then he spurted, three times, her hand stroking it out of him again and again, the pale fluid splashing on his chest and stomach, before he relaxed totally and sank back into the water, sitting down again, quiet, exhausted. Then she let go of him, and he raised his face up to her and kissed her.

Thinking of that, Stevie had masturbated twice yesterday afternoon, and again today. Even remembering it, knowing it was a fantasy, made her restless. She knew it hadn't happened, probably wouldn't happen. Or if it did, had, their relationship—for what it was—would be over. Or would it? If only she could be more patient; if only she didn't force herself on him, but allowed him to come to her. But would he?

He did seem to like her and to want her company. At least he didn't avoid her. That must mean something, no? Take today for example. She'd been coming down the ramp from the deck of her family's house, on her way to the village to do grocery shopping. When she reached the boardwalk, she saw Jonathan putting out large, shiny, plastic garbage bags, explaining to her that it was refuse collection day. He'd been wearing a different pair of shorts, pale blue ones with deep slashed pockets on their sides that hugged his hips, this time topped by a dark blue Lacoste shirt. His hair seemed more curly, more unkempt than usual, his eyes slightly puffy and veiled, as though he hadn't slept enough last night. But he'd smiled at her and been friendly, and asked where she was going. When she told him, he said he had errands to do too: could he accompany her? Stevie had waited on his front deck, looking at the wonderful view of the ocean as he went inside to make a fast grocery list and get his wallet. She looked down at his lined music paper, filled with illegible scrawls and notations that seemed almost like cuneiform. She'd wondered what to say about the evening before; but as she had already turned it into a fairly satisfying fantasy, she couldn't bring herself to spoil it by saying anything about it to him. If he brought it up, of course… He came out, fingers or a brush run through his hair, his beard slicked down, slightly damp so that tiny droplets of water gathered between curls like dew on a lawn. And they had walked and talked, chatting, friendly, Jonathan telling her how the boys had eaten him out of house and home but what a good distraction they had been from the grind of his work. Then she had felt the snag to her toe and looked down.

"Cab, ma'am," Jonathan said.

She realized she'd been daydreaming. She looked up to see Jonathan pulling a little red Radio Flyer wagon with two bags of groceries standing in it.

"I couldn't," she said. "I'll break it."

"Step in," he said, and came to help lift her into it.

"I'm too heavy."

"We moved the stereo equipment in this," he said. "Come on— that weighed more than you do."

When she was settled in the wagon, he placed the two bags of groceries in front of her. Her bandaged foot stuck out over the railing. She didn't feel like a child. She felt like an oversize adult playing a child's game.

"Present," he said, and handed her a long, green tissue paper cone.

"What is it?"

"Open it."

She tore the top of the paper and exposed a brilliant coral- and wine-colored orchid, with dewlaps of speckled red on white; it was as soft as satin. It smelled luscious and vaguely familiar.

"That's for being a patient invalid," he said.

He went in front and lifted up the handle.

"Hold on," he said, and began to pull.

When they arrived at the place on their boardwalk where her ramp began, she started to get out of the wagon.

"Stay put," he said. "You're my guest for dinner tonight. Remember what Barbara said about you having to stay off your foot for a while. Looks like you're going to be pampered a little bit. So you might as well get used to it."

She began to argue, but he didn't listen. He pulled the wagon up to his house and onto the back deck, helped her out, set her into a chaise longue, then unpacked the groceries.

It was only several hours later, still in his house, when she was gingerly stepping into the shower before dinner, that she knew what the fragrance was she had smelled so strongly in the orchid: it was herself.

CHAPTER THIRTEEN

It was odd the way she slept, her body half on its side, curled against his, or against the barrier of sheets and light blankets he'd thrown off in his sleep. The same kind of sleeping that Artie and Ken did, as though even in her sleep she had to be sure he was there. She didn't snore either, although once in a while he would hear a slight gasp, half a sigh, as though she'd remembered something sad in a dream. She did move around while sleeping, unlike Jonathan, who went to sleep flat on his back, his hands at his sides, or folded in front, and woke up exactly in that position, hours later. Daniel used to say he would be an easy job for the mortician if he died in his sleep. Not Stevie. Jonathan would half awaken to find her head on his chest, her legs entwined in his, the fingers of one of his hands threaded through hers. She dreamed too. Jonathan almost never dreamed, or if he did, seldom remembered doing so later. Daniel dreamed too, on occasion. He would waken Jonathan sometimes with his somnambulistic battles. "Hey!" Jonathan would have to shout and Daniel would awaken embarrassed, or surprised. One time, Daniel had begun to strike out in his sleep, and Jonathan had to protect himself, which was difficult since Daniel was so much larger, and finally he'd struck back. Daniel had come to then, and they'd both stayed awake until dawn, trying to explain to each other what had happened, what flaw had occurred in their communication.

Now the telephone was going to ring. He'd asked Daniel to call later. Stevie liked to sleep late. But so far Dan hadn't gone along with this. Slave to habit as he was. Or to having his own way. Jonathan was never certain which. At least Jonathan had turned off the phone in the bedrooms, so it only rang distantly, in the kitchen, too far away for it to bother her. There it went!

He pulled himself out of bed, pulled on a pair of shorts, walked sleepily out, closing the bedroom door, going out into the light of another splendidly sunny day, opening two glass doors to catch the fresh ocean morning, then opening the back deck glass doors, for the odor of hot-leaved Swedish ivy.

"Hello," he said into the receiver. Then, without even listening to what the overseas operator was saying, "Yes. I'll accept the call."

"You sound sleepy."

"I told you I was sleeping later," Jonathan said. "It has something to do with the change of seasons. Hold on, will you. I want to heat up some coffee."

Daniel began talking, as he usually did, this time about the scriptwriters, who wouldn't accept the least bit of criticism. "They all think they're fucking George Bernard Shaw or something," Daniel insisted. "And he could have used a good editor, too, if you ask me." Then about the actors in the first two films, some of whom were terrific in their parts, and others awful. "Sods. Bleedings sods," Daniel called them—he'd already assimilated all the argot on the set.

"That's probably what they call you, when you aren't there to hear," Jonathan said. "With better cause."

"What's that supposed to mean?"

"Well, don't you know what a sod is? It's a sodomite."

"Oh?" Daniel said in that small, tight voice, by which he expressed correction or knowledge imparted, as though he were doing a favor by listening, by learning. Then he sailed on about the producers.

Jonathan listened for a long time without further interruption or comment. He sipped his coffee; he pulled the phone outside onto the deck, where the sun had burned off a light mist, and where he could see the water on both sides of the island sparkling with the fractured intensity of a Monet seascape.

"So, when he gave me that line," Daniel said, "I told him…" Jonathan uh-hmmed and uh-huhed a bit to show he was still on the line. But he wasn't. He was thinking about act two of *Lady and the Falcon,* where only last night, in a burst of surprising creativity, he had added an entirely new number for Fiammetta's father, a complaint of great complexity and humor: the old man's list of how his daughter was driving him to distraction. He'd called up his collaborator, Barry, and first outlined it very carefully, explaining how, without this break, the show would run from one relatively quiet number to another rather somber one—the chiding chorus of the women against Fiammetta's whimsicality. Surprisingly, Barry was amenable. Even more astonishing, after having Jonathan's ad-libbed lyrics read to him only three times, he made a half dozen changes, and agreed to the inclusion of the new song.

Finally Daniel stopped, interrupting himself to say, "Aren't you awake yet?"

"Uh-huh," Jonathan answered.

"You don't sound it. Are you sick or something?"

"I'm fine. I'm just waking up. I was up very late working last night, Dan."

The other end of the line was silent, then, "Is anything wrong there? Barry or Saul or anyone giving you a hard time?"

"On the contrary. They're being perfect angels."

"The composing going all right?"

"Terrific. That's why I was up late last night. That's why I'm still sleepy. What is this, anyway? A cross-examination?"

"You don't sound right," Daniel said firmly.

"How in the hell can you tell? You're the one doing all the talking!"

"Something *is* wrong," said Daniel; and his conviction irritated Jonathan even more than his refusal to listen.

"Nothing's wrong," Jonathan said calmly.

"I know you, Jonathan Lash. And I say something's wrong.

You're sick, or angry with me, or something is off with your score, or someone is giving you trouble. It's not the kids, is it?"

"Nothing is wrong," Jonathan said with Antarctic coolness, aware that Daniel would interpret this, too, as proof of what he was asserting, as he would if Jonathan were calm or angry or insanely raging. Damn Dan! "Go on," he said, attempting to alter his tone to one of greater warmth. "You were talking about Heather and Tony."

There was another short silence, then Daniel did go on talking about the filming problems, but he never seemed as unself-consciously glib as before his question. Before he hung up, he wanted to leave a number where he would be in the next few hours.

"What for?" Jonathan asked. "So you'll fly over and pat my wrists? How inane!"

"Well," Daniel waffled. "Maybe it really just is a case of your getting up on the wrong side of the bed, after all."

"Hey, Daniel," Jonathan said in an urgent, conspiratorial whisper.

Daniel answered back warily, "What?"

"Screw yourself," Jonathan said, and hung up. "Wasn't that mature," he said to himself, and sighed.

He brought the phone back into the kitchen, thought of taking it off the hook, then decided against it. If Daniel called again, he'd let it ring. He wouldn't answer it. Then he went back out onto the deck, his coffee mug refilled, with a cigarette, and a sun visor against the glare.

Not much birdsong this late in the month. In May and June the goldfinches and greenfiches would chirrup, cavorting through the bushes surrounding the deck, zooming in and out of the leaves. Most of the butterflies were gone too. Only a few, languid, aged ones still slowly sailed by—specimens that would never complete the migration to their spawning grounds south. Very few monarchs had passed this year compared to last September, when there had been thousands of them every day for three weeks, clouds of them for a few days: afterward lovely, rich-colored corpses everywhere— from old age, accidents, head winds, and fatigue. This year he'd seen one dead monarch on the surf, its wing caught in the grip of a sand crab; both creatures dead. Fascinated, he'd looked at them entangled in their awful dance of death and fate, and remembered Robert Frost's poem "Design," that haunting, morbid sonnet. Later on, he'd thought about them, thought that if he were to take a photo of them, someone would surely accuse him of being surrealist or symbolist—and whichever, take him to task for being so obvious about it. Yet it had happened naturally. Nature, life, accident, design, fate had been responsible, not he. And that could never be cheapened.

Of course the swallows were more numerous this summer, as though making up for the dearth of butterflies. Like little Phantom jets, twisting and spinning over the houses and down again, their wings turned vertically, they swerved between telephone wires only inches apart at incredible speeds, around poles, over hedges, and never seemed to have accidents. They appeared to take real pleasure in flying, unlike so many other birds, who flew unconsciously: the hummingbird on its rotaries pecking at the stamen of a flower, tiny, like a wind-up Japanese toy. He was always astonished at hummingbirds, but he loved swallows for their love of flying.

He'd been an idiot, of course, to let Dan hear he was annoyed. He'd never hear the end of it now. It was his own fault, naturally. He'd fallen right into the trap: Daniel's tidy little irritation trap, set especially for him, as carefully constructed as a black widow's. The bastard! He was incorrigible. Even from across the Atlantic, fresh from some boy harlot's bed, he'd managed to pull off this number on Jonathan with unerring aim and skill. He'd do anything to avert suspicion from himself, of course, to cover up his own tracks. God knew, even half listening to him as Jonathan had been, he'd picked up enough key words and hinting modulations to figure out what Daniel was up to over there, as clearly as though his life were a television sitcom that had been going on for years, where one has tuned in for one program midway.

Jonathan went back into the house, opened the bedroom door, and watched Stevie sleep. She'd moved almost entirely onto the area he'd just gotten up from fifteen minutes ago. For an instant, he thought of going back to bed, of awakening on the other side of her and letting her be surprised by it as he avoided mentioning it, instead covering her with touches and kisses. Then the private world of her sleep dissuaded him. He stood sipping his coffee, watching her, noting details.

Would she be surprised? Perhaps not. She seemed to take an awful lot of things that astounded him for granted. Such as the fact that she'd been sleeping with him, in his bed, making love with him, for four days now.

He remembered quite clearly how it happened, could work out minisecond by minisecond what had led them finally together: her hurt toe, the ride in the wagon back here, her going into the shower while he fixed dinner, how he suddenly thought he'd heard her fall and shut off the burner and run into the bathroom, thrown open the door, expecting to having to lift a bloodied unconscious girl and begin dialing for the police to send over an ambulance or suddenly use a towel as a tourniquet or begin pumping her arms and chest to restore breathing. She was sitting on the edge of the tub, nude, both hands up to her long hair as she toweled it dry, one foot forward, the little bandage on her toe soaked, the look of surprise on her face, his stammer, his attempted explanation, then how he'd stopped, gone over to her, lifted her off her perch, carried her into the bedroom, tossed her onto his bed, and without even removing his own clothing, mounted her.

Now she was turned over on her stomach, yet not completely, with one hip tilted up, and one buttock uncovered, soft as a newly molded scoop of peach sherbet.

What a lovely creature, he thought, almost not real. Her youth accounted for much, he knew. He suspected that if she were a boy, he wouldn't have waited as long as he had to make love to her; he would have succumbed in a day or so. Even so, it was her androgynous youth that kept him interested in her. Her exposed skin didn't so much reflect light as it absorbed it, absorbed it and seemed to hold that light inside it, allowing it to softly glow. Her facial skin was like that too—as though the various layers of epidermis hadn't yet decided which was outer and which inner. Even through a tan, he could see a rosy infusion begin to manifest itself on her cheeks—or paleness draw all color suddenly from her forehead. It was amazing how young she was, really, only a few years older than Ken. She'd come to him like some kind of not quite human creature—a nymph or seashore deity—and had installed herself rapidly into his affections, his arms, his life, his schedule, and his attentions.

And she was easy to have around. She was completely responsive to him yet considerate of his need for privacy too—something Daniel had never come close to achieving. He'd already grown used to forgetting she was even in the room with him, she was so quiet, sitting for the longest time as he composed, for example. He would get up from his table or from the piano, facing another choice, another tiny block to his progress. He would step outside, tap his pen against the glass door for a rhythm, grumble, even walk out onto the beach, before sitting down again to continue. Often he would go find something to nibble on in the kitchen, or suddenly remember to make a phone call. Meanwhile Stevie would be reading, or working on some sort of list in a notebook with marbled covers she'd picked up in the grocery store, or slowly making dinner. And yet, if he wanted her company—no matter how instant, how seemingly arbitrary the wish—she was ready to go out for a swim, to take a stroll along the beach, or on the boardwalks of the increasingly empty resort, now that it was late September, and midweek. Then she would suddenly disappear back into her family's house for several hours, without any explanation, and as suddenly reappear with an idea for lunch, or a question about something she was reading. She read voraciously these days, surpassing even Daniel in the month before he went to London, when he seemed to have emptied half the city's public libraries of their biographies and histories of the early days of the American presidency. There were gaps all over the bookcase from her rapid selections. Bright Stevie, pleasant, and intelligent too.

She rolled over a bit in bed and looked up at him.

"Getting up?" she asked.

"Already up," he said. He held out the half-full coffee mug to her.

She reached for it, sitting up in bed. He sat down on the edge of the bed and watched her sip. She lapped it up like a puppy, all the while looking not at the mug, but at him.

"The phone rang," he explained.

She didn't ask who it was. She didn't say, "Oh, Dan again," or anything like that. That was part of Stevie, part of their thing together, whatever one might call it—relationship, affair, love; he didn't put it into words. Whatever it was, it was designed of a fine network of questions not asked, and so not requiring answers; of problems not discussed, and so not recognized as problems; of difficulties never alluded to, and so invisible; of differences never mentioned, possibilities discouraged, futures disdained. Delicate as a spider's web, that fragile and complex was their togetherness. Not too delicate for sex, certainly, but far too delicate for emotions. He had to admire her for allowing that. It belied a maturity he'd not expected, and expressed a sensibility he'd hardly anticipated. All ideas of shotgun weddings were vanished, made to seem ridiculous. She was quite the lady in waiting, she was so beautifully mannered. Jonathan had almost forgotten how finely tuned a woman's courtesy could be.

"Want your own cup?" he asked. "There's more."

She shook her head no, and sank back into the pillows. "I dreamed again. About talking to my parents."

"Was it better or worse than the real thing?"

"I can't remember. I mean in the dream it was grim. But it's been so long in real life."

He let that go. Why stop it?

"Weren't you talking to them yesterday?" he asked. She'd been on the phone for a while.

"That was a friend from school. Rose."

"They know you're here, don't they?"

"Here?" she asked, looking around the room. They both laughed. "They know I'm at Sea Mist. I've sent them a postcard."

"So Rose reports in for you?"

"No. She's at school. She doesn't speak to them."

He was suddenly concerned. "You mean you haven't talked

to them since you've come out here? Not even to tell them you're alive?" He realized he sounded like a parent himself, which hadn't been his intention.

"Especially not to tell them I'm alive," she said. "I want them to think I'm suffering beautifully, against a backdrop of crashing waves."

She frowned. "Do you think I ought to?"

"Maybe not," he hedged. "Maybe the fact that you dreamed about them is enough."

"Or maybe that's why I dreamed about them?"

"Maybe."

"Do you think I ought to call them?" she asked timidly.

He didn't answer. He felt he'd already gone too far in advising, admitting she had a life beside this one, four days old, with him. He hated admitting it, because it meant he had to admit he had one too.

"Jonathan?"

"I don't know."

She looked up surprised.

"You asked me something?" he said. "You said my name."

"Did I?" she said and relaxed back into the pillows. From her slight perplexity just then, he realized she'd said his name not to continue questioning him, but unconsciously, as though it were a talisman, or phrase of prayer. *"Salva me."* Fiammetta of Florence would do such a thing. Not Giustina, the servant girl, the realist, but the lovely, spoiled, idealistic aristocrat Fiammetta—destroyer of wooers' wits and hopes with her madly exaggerated image of a falcon that never existed. She would whisper the falcon's hallowed name unconsciously in her garden, between the lemon trees, and Don Farnace would try to win her hand, cunningly, by overhearing her and calling his own ragged gyrfalcon by the same name.

Being with Stevie had helped him review those characters, revising them almost daily, it seemed. He also came to understand their aunts and sisters and grandmothers, and girl friends too. Stevie could be a little girl, then in a twinkling—"ein Augenblick," Heine would say, the flick of an eyelash—she would be a mature woman, or a more distanced older woman, speaking and acting from decades of experience. He'd already written two new choruses and rewritten another madrigal commentary in the show into all woman pieces, divided those into various parts he'd seen in her, and come up with a complexity of harmonics and tone he really liked. She was an inspiration too: a little Seven Sisters Erato.

"It's sunny out," he said. "Sunny and hot. Surprised?"

"Glad."

"Why don't you get up and go to the beach? I'll join you in a little."

She began to get up out of bed, and he was moved to take her right there, not to let her up, to cover her with himself, to have her warm and soft and receptive from sleep.

He let it sweep over him, then let her pass him, and went and stood as she walked into the bathroom and turned on the shower.

This was crazy, he thought. It couldn't go on much longer. It couldn't increase so continually, could it, this desire to have her all the time? His head was filled with thoughts. His shorts sprouted an erection.

He saw her get into the shower and wave, then heard the fine spray of the shower go on, then blast with greater force, its regular pulsations broken now by flesh under it.

In the bathroom, he slipped off his shorts and got in the shower too.

She began to lather his skin with a sponge and soap. She was very meticulous, very thorough. He kept on slowly bringing her hands down to his front.

"Here?" she said. "Now? I thought it had passed a moment ago, when I was in bed?"

"Don't be so sassy," he said. "Besides, what do you have against being clean?"

Leaning against her, he let the water shoot between their faces.

Later on, on the beach, she started to laugh without any apparent cause, and then blushed to explain: "You're taking away all of my fantasies. This morning, in the shower, that was one. What will I do when none are left?"

He didn't answer her; certainly not to say anything similar to her, for that would be an untruth, wouldn't it? The last thing they could tolerate was untruth.

CHAPTER FOURTEEN

The letter from Bill was short, but really rather touching: it was sad without being sentimental and only evoked her guilt over mistreating him a little bit. She wasn't surprised he'd sent it: she was surprised that's all he'd done. She'd really expected to see him waiting for her on her deck, or inside the house one weekend afternoon when she returned from the beach.

There was no other mail for her, but there were two more letters for Jonathan.

Barbara didn't say anything; she didn't even raise an eyebrow when Stevie asked for Mr. Lash's mail. She simply handed it to her, and went back to her reading. The two little girls were asleep in the back of the shaded, cool room. Not a mention of Stevie's foot she'd helped mend, nothing to make Stevie feel she had to explain why she was picking up his mail. Nothing.

She went out to the harbor and sat down, and reread Bill's letter. It remained noncommittal and touching.

What was odd was that she'd also dreamed about Bill last night. He was in the room when she met her parents, sitting on the sofa, not saying a word.

She'd only begun to think of Bill Tierney again in the last few days—in fact, since she'd begun sleeping with Jonathan. That was one of the odd side effects of their actual physical contact she'd so much desired. The following morning she'd almost called him Bill once, and when she thought about it later, she knew she felt disloyal to Bill.

There were other side effects too: a sudden cessation of tension, as though all she'd really needed was to get laid, horrible as that was to contemplate. Not a reduction of passion, but rather an evening out of the sharpness of her desire. It would rise to meet his own passion, naturally. But was otherwise dormant. She was content. She had gotten something she wanted, and that made a huge difference since it seemed that for the last year or so she'd gotten nothing she wanted—hadn't even known what that might be. But poor Bill! He was her past, and he already knew it. She hadn't meant to break so badly, so fumblingly; but she supposed it was better this way.

She would call Bill when she returned to town, of course; she would make it clear that what he suspected was true. She would ask Rose how to do it; surely Rose Heywood had broken off with lovers before and could tell her how to do it graciously. She suspected Rose would be wonderful at such things; she was positively Jamesian at times in her dealings with the students—her mixture of hidden disdain and complex compassion made her enviable and aloof.

Stevie folded the note and put it in her pocket and went off to do her grocery shopping.

As she was on her way home, passing along the edge of the little harbor, the blond man stopped unloading the tall, dull gray canisters of natural gas all the houses at Sea Mist used and said, "What did you do to your foot?"

"Tore it on a nail," she answered. She'd been thinking about dinner later with Jonathan, candlelit in his dining room, the fire going perhaps in the other room. She was only half-conscious of the man inquiring. But now he lifted himself out of the flatboat and onto the deck beside her.

"Did you get shots for it?" he asked.

He was surprisingly young. She'd thought him mid-thirties or fortyish before. Now that he was so close, she saw that he was only a few years older than she, his face hidden behind a deep tan and a wild blond and brown beard.

"Barbara at the post office took care of it. She put some kind of antiseptic on it," Stevie said, then continued on.

He caught up with her. "Maybe you shouldn't be walking on it."

"It's all right. It happened a while ago. It's almost healed up."

He continued parallel to her around the harbor.

"I could carry your package for you. That must be pressure on it."

"No, thanks," she said, then went along to where the main boardwalk began, and continued walking.

"I have a key for the truck," he said, still alongside her. "I can give you a ride."

She was feeling annoyed now: he *was* persistent. Perhaps she'd sensed that as a potentiality in him right away, that first day here at Sea Mist. Maybe that's why she'd placed him lurking in the darkened corners of her family's ill-lit house during the night of the thunderstorm.

"It's not far."

"You're Jerry Locke's sister, aren't you?"

"So?"

"We were friends. Jerry and I. A couple of summers ago," he said.

How transparent he was being, she thought, to take that line.

"Really! Well, then you're the only male friend of Jerry's I ever met out here."

"What?" He was confused.

"I believe it was said of my brother that he'd sleep with your wife as soon as shake your hand here in Sea Mist."

He became more confused than ever. "I don't have a wife," he protested.

Jonathan would have laughed at her quip, gently, with irony. The poor thing... "Forget it," she said.

"Wait a minute. My name's Matt. What's yours?"

He wasn't going to leave her alone.

"Why don't you call me Jerry's sister?" she said. Lord, she was halfway home and he still wasn't letting up.

"Do you mind if I walk you home?" he asked, stopping and touching her arm.

"Yes," she said.

"You mean it's okay?"

"No. I mean, yes, I do mind."

She'd meant it to be clear. It was. His face colored over, a deep unhealthy red that she took at first for blushing, until she saw it was equally composed of anger.

"Just because you go to college, that doesn't make you better than me," he said, thickly, loudly.

"I never said I was."

"Well, you sure act it!"

"If you'd behave like a gentleman, I wouldn't have to act it."

"I'm not a gentleman! I'm a ferry hauler!" he said, pride and shame mingled in it. "But I don't have to be a gentleman. I'm honest. And I'm clean. And I know what this is for," he said, suddenly gripping the crotch of his pants.

His intensity, his roughness, and especially that last gesture startled her. For a second she was certain he was going to strike her, knock the groceries out of her hands, grab her, and pull her off the walk into the yard of an unoccupied house, and there beat and rape her. He was trembling, on the edge of something, some kind of violence or impulse or breakdown, she didn't know which. If only Jonathan were here. He'd offered to come with her. Or if only... who? Her father? Lord Bracknell? Or Bill Tierney? Those fools would rip this guy apart first and ask questions later.

She was alone now, on her own, as she had wished. She had to try to handle this disturbed man herself, or scream and run and attempt to find some kind of help from him among the dozens of vacant houses surrounding them. Thinking that helped her somewhat: she really only had one choice. Her panic subsided.

"Hey, Matt," she said, trying to put all the sympathy she could gather into her words, "I didn't say you didn't know what to do."

"You sure acted like it." Stubborn.

She tried reasoning with him: "Why should it make any difference to you what I think or act like?"

That stumped him for a second. Then, honest as he said he was, he blurted out, "Because I like you."

"I like you too, Matt," she said. "But I don't worry about how you think or act."

"I mean," he began hesitantly, the anger ebbing, the embarrassment continuing, "I like you a lot."

"Well, thanks, Matt. But you know, I'm seeing someone."

"He didn't come out here with you."

"I'm *still* seeing him. I'm not leading you on, am I?" she asked. "Is that what you think?"

More hesitantly, "No. I guess not."

"Is that the kind of woman you think I am, to be seeing someone and to go around leading on other guys?" She hoped this would disarm him a bit, allow his confused ideas to settle, rather than incite him further.

Hesitantly again, "I guess not."

"Good!" she said, more brightly this time. "Then why don't we be friendly, instead of arguing over nothing. All right?"

He didn't answer.

"Would you want someone coming on to your girlfriend?"

"I don't have a girlfriend."

"I'm sorry, Matt," and she meant that. He'd taken his hand off his crotch; both of them hung, large and potentially dangerous, next to his sides. He seemed so young now. Stevie felt so strong with him, strong in a way she'd never really felt before, not even with Jonathan.

"Do you want to relax and talk awhile?" she asked. "I'm a little tired. My foot is hurting again. Why don't we sit here and talk?"

She sat on the boardwalk, making certain to place the bag of groceries next to herself, between them, then gestured for him to join her. They were out in the open, on the main walk, surely the most public spot around, although she hadn't seen any passersby since she'd left the harbor. He slowly joined her, moving a bit closer than she would have liked, pressing up against the groceries. She put out her feet, so they dangled over the sand. Longer, lankier, Matt sat next to her, looking at her, then down at the sand, still embarrassed. She hoped she was doing the right thing. But it must be right: he seemed relaxed, and her panic had subsided to an occasional shiver around her heart.

"You have very nice eyes," she said. They were blue-gray like bay waters on a stormy day. Uncertain eyes.

He looked down at his feet, silent. Evidently he wasn't comfortable.

"So! You're a ferry hauler. I always wondered what that was called."

"That's what they call us. You know, in the businesses here and on the other side." His voice was still sulky.

"Do you live with your family on the other side?"

"Just my dad and my brother. He's a mechanic for the Long Island Railroad. My dad worked for the railroad too. He's retired now. Paralyzed. My mom's dead…" His voice trailed away.

She asked another question; then another. Little by little, Matt began telling her about himself and his family. She heard about his hard, bleak childhood, a life without luxuries, without promise, a life of hand-me-downs and pride in just managing to get by. He'd had little schooling, had gone to work early on and was still working hard. She got the impression it wasn't very different from Barbara's life. No wonder they hated and envied the summer people—who had money, who vacationed here three or four months a year without suffering because of that, and who provided them with work, food, clothing, infrequently a new bike for their children or a new boat for their livelihood. Stevie found she had to draw Matt's words out of him, he was so reticent. It was clear that he was bitter. Only when he'd begun work as a ferry hauler three years before and come to see the summer people's lives—their yachts, their limousines picking them up on the mainland, their houses here, their expensive purchases, had he suddenly realized how much he was lacking—and would probably always lack. It was easy for her to be attentive to him— now that she'd gotten over her initial terror she was fascinated. He was a boy who not only lacked material things, he seemed most to lack love: whereas her life was drenched in love, cushioned by it, burdened with it even, on all sides. Yes, that was what her dream this morning had reminded her, how many obligations of affection she had—to her family, to Bill, to her friends at school, and now to Jonathan. It was too much, not too little she suffered from. And now she was starting to make them suffer for giving it to her. Only Jonathan was exempt; theirs was such a new, and special kind of love: with no attachments, no debts. But the others! Rose and the girls at Smith missed her; Bill missed her; she knew her mother must be sorry by now she'd given her the keys to the summer house. Stevie hadn't meant for any of this to happen.

Matt was winding down, finishing his narration. His words came more slowly, he paused more between sentences. He told her about a boat he wanted to buy—to become an independent ferry hauler. He mentioned how he sometimes thought of just picking up and leaving, going west, to the Rockies, to Seattle, perhaps to become a logger. He heard there was a good living in that, constant work, and beautiful women.

"In California," she said, "the women are very beautiful. Maybe you ought to do that, Matt. Move out west. You like the sun and the outdoors and the water. Why not go where you have those all year round. Who knows, maybe your woman is waiting for you out there."

"My woman?"

"Your intended," she said firmly. "As I'm intended for someone else." Calmly enough said, but in the middle of saying it, the question within it had almost silenced her: Who *was* her intended? Bill? Jonathan? Someone else?

"You really think so?" he asked. He evidently liked the idea.

"Why not? And how are you going to find out, unless you try, right?"

"Maybe," hesitantly. Then, "They really do get me down here. My dad and brother. Especially in the winter."

"No winter in California," she said.

"I think I ought to apologize for everything I said before." He looked down at his feet again.

"You don't have to, Matt."

"Just talking here with you makes me feel better," and he cracked a little smile. His lips seemed parched, his teeth yellowish, bad for someone so young. "Even dreams…"

"If you have a dream, you should follow it," she said. "If you don't follow it, you'll never know if you can really have it or not."

His whole face opened up at that.

Stevie was surprised at her own words, which had just slipped out of her. She was wondering where they'd come from. Did she really believe what she said? And if not, why had she said it? Merely to comfort him? Then what was her own dream? Was it this, being strong, being independent, not relying on others, being able to sit down and talk to someone like Matt, someone disturbed, in need of another person, and even help him?

It did make her feel good. She wasn't tired by it, wasn't at all bored, she was fascinated by the glimpses into his life she'd received—touched by his revelation of a possible future for himself—as though it were a gift to her. Maybe this was what she wanted. And all she would have to do was to follow her ideal, and the rest would follow in time, a man, or a family, or something else—friends, a career, doing something useful.

It rang through her body like a gong suddenly struck. She felt so elated, she thought she might be hyperventilating.

Matt chose that moment to stand up on the boardwalk and offer to help her up. He thanked her, apologized again, backed off, thanked her again, then turned and began to walk away, back toward the harbor. Was it her imagination, or was he walking with a lighter, springier step, as though he'd dropped a load off his shoulders?

Still stunned by what this odd meeting had told her about herself, Stevie walked home slowly, and turned onto the ramp to her family's house. She was halfway up it, before she realized her mistake.

"Damn!" she said, stopped on the walkway. "That's the second time today about my parents. I'm going to have to do something about that."

When she entered the lovers' house a few minutes later—how

apt, how prescient her bestowal of the name had been!—Jonathan was at his desk. He looked up from his composing.

"You sure had a good walk," he said.

"Why do you say that?"

"You look as though you're glowing."

She restrained her excitement, and said, "Something wonderful happened to me. Terrifying at first. Even a little terrifying right now. But wonderful!"

His kind dark eyes looked at her without surprise.

"Would you like to share it with me?" he asked. Who but Jonathan would ask such a heavenly question, she asked herself; certainly not Bill Tierney, who would mutter, "That's nice," or something else equally inane.

"Yes! But…" How could she share it with him? A part of it—the most unknowable part of it, the X-factor, was Jonathan himself. "I don't know," she faltered. "I don't know where to begin. Do you mind if I don't share it with you?"

"If it's that private, no problem." He got up and took the grocery bag from her, bringing it into the kitchen where he began laying her purchases out on the counter. "How about a cup of tea and a game of Scrabble?" he asked.

"You really don't mind?" she asked. She had to know.

"You'll tell me when you're ready." Then, looking at the groceries, "God, what a huge container of milk. And you mean to say you really drink it like that? Straight? Without coffee or brandy or anything in it?" He shuddered in mock disgust, and she had to laugh.

"I have to warn you," she said, as he got out the Scrabble board, "I cheat."

"Oh! Not another one!" he said, then seemed to have been struck by a thought. He became suddenly silent, even clouded over.

He'd thought of Daniel, Stevie knew: Daniel cheated at Scrabble too. Hell! The lovely filigree of their being together was coming apart for him too.

Chapter Fifteen

He was walking down the street in a foreign city, an old city. It was daylight, but he was unsure of the hour. The light was so strange—so bright and yet without glare—he couldn't tell whether it was late morning or just before sunset. Whatever time it was, it bathed the surrounding buildings in an odd light, as though they were being illuminated for a film to be shot. Colonnades to his left seemed endlessly repetitive. A tall building of some sort with a crenellated roof visible loomed on his other side. The paving stones under his feet were unusually large, lightly pitted, pale gray; gutters—like half pipes set into their surface—ran along them: real gutters. It was a very old city. When he finally reached the end of the two long buildings, he was in a large, empty plaza. He realized he must be in some Italian city—Florence or Siena. There was a lovely little Romanesque-style church to one side; and in the middle of the plaza, a statue on a tall pedestal. Perseus? Suddenly he heard a telephone ringing. He looked all around him in the plaza, thinking he was near a phone kiosk, but there was none—no other structures but the apse of the church and the statue—David?—on the pedestal. Could it be ringing from where he'd emerged? From behind those colonnades? Or, perhaps, ahead of him, inside the church? It was somehow extremely important that he reach the phone and answer it, desperately important. But there was no one on the street to ask where it was. He began running, first through the colonnades, then, when these only showed him an endless gray brick wall, across the street to the tall building, which had many doors. All of them were locked. Finally he dashed back into the plaza, and toward the church. He flung open the huge, cast bronze, carefully balanced doors, and rushed inside. Except for a flock of geese waddling across the dark, musty, tiled floor, and the distorted light filtering down through oddly colored high windows, he could see nothing inside. He edged back out again, into the plaza. The phone had suddenly stopped ringing, and he cursed himself for being unable to reach it. Then he heard her voice—and he knew it was Fiammetta calling him. There she was, at the other end of the plaza; she'd just come over a curved footbridge—were they in Venice suddenly?—running toward him. She wore a Nile green gown, embroidered with pearls at her throat and wrists, the sleeves slashed to explode out bunches of white satin. Her hair was the gold of an antique coin, fashionably plucked so her wide, lovely brow was higher than it ought to be. She charged right into his arms, shaking him...shaking him...

He woke up. Stevie was on the bed, almost astride him, shaking him awake.

"It's Dan," she said. "He's on the phone. From London."

"Dan?" He sat up suddenly, awakened totally. "What time is it?"

It was barely midnight. He'd only been asleep a half hour.

"I had to get it," she said apologetically. "Even out there it was keeping me awake. It just rang and rang, then started ringing again. I'm sorry, Jonathan. If I'd thought it was Dan... I thought it must be someone else. Some emergency or something."

He held her close.

"It's all right. I'll take it. Try to get some sleep."

He'd awakened as thoroughly as though there were a burglar in the house, or a murdering intruder. He jumped out of bed, rolling her over him, and pulled on a pair of shorts. Daniel hadn't called this morning: hadn't called since Jonathan had hung up on him. Well, he would have to be dealt with sometime. Why not now?

"Try to go to sleep," he said, closing the bedroom door behind him.

"Jonathan?" she called.

"What?"

"Nothing." Then: "I was going to ask you not to fight. Please?"

"I won't," he said.

"Liar!"

"Am I that transparent to you?"

She had to think about that. "Not really," she admitted.

"Go to sleep!"

"I'll try," she said, unconvinced.

He went to the phone in the living room, picked it up, heard nothing on the other end, and wondered if they'd lost the connection. He extracted a cigarette from the package on the table and lighted it.

"Jonathan? You there?" Daniel's voice sounded odd.

Here goes, Jonathan thought. "Hi, Dan." Breezily. "What's with the phone call? Trouble?"

"Who was that who answered the phone?" Dan asked, equally airily. So that was how it was going to be played.

"The Locke girl. Stevie. You remember her. From across the way. Lady Bracknell's ward." Said as easily as though they were talking about someone not seen in months.

"So…?" Dan inquired, as though over a Campari cocktail on the Via Veneto.

"She came out here to be away from her parents. She's going through a few crises. Undergoing pressures."

"I see. Crises. Pressures."

"That's right. You know the usual postadolescent stuff. Whether to finish college or go to work. Whether to become independent or not. Kid stuff." He puffed on the cigarette theatrically.

Without missing a beat, or changing an inflection in his voice, Dan asked, "How long have you been sleeping with her?"

A nice turn. Bravo! Jonathan thought.

"About a week. No. Not quite." Let's be civilized, his tone said.

"Not quite a week?" Slightly surprised—so the crumpets don't come with the tea today. Only scones. That kind of question. "Well, that must have made her forget her little crises. Unless," urbanely added, "it created a new one."

"I don't think so," Jonathan said, letting the smoke drift out of his mouth, à la Ronald Colman in God knew what awful movie. "Of course, I can't really claim to have helped her any."

"I'm certain you did. You're always so good with the little human touches."

This farce of cynicism and hypocrisy was beginning to pall on Jonathan. It wasn't getting them anywhere. They knew they could play it for hours if they chose: they were well enough matched for it. Why bother? He'd leave the phone for a minute on some pretext. Dan would naturally assume he was going to Stevie, and reporting their talk to her. When he picked up the receiver again, Daniel would be furious. Then it would really begin.

"Hold on a second, will you, Dan?" he said, left the phone without waiting for an answer, and went to the window wall, one panel of which he moved aside so only the screen remained.

Dew spangled the screen's mesh already. Farther away a green meteorite dove through the night sky toward the horizon, exploding in a tiny emerald and white puff. It was chilly out. He'd better put on a shirt.

When he got back to the phone it was silent. He thought he heard a sob. Oh, no! That wasn't what he wanted on a transatlantic call. Concerned, he asked. "Daniel? You there? What's going on?"

Daniel's answer was calm, collected, showing Jonathan he'd been wrong about the sob. "Here? Nothing wrong. A little postadolescent crisis, perhaps. Perhaps a little realization that I've been awake until five thirty in the morning, Greenwich time, worrying about my lover in New York who's been acting a little bit unlike himself, while he's busily screwing some young girl. Aside from that, nothing. Nothing important, certainly."

"I'm not going to say I'm sorry."

"Heaven forbid!" The first outburst. Then, calmer, "Sorry, babe. The strain, you know. The distance and all." Then, "Are you in love with her?"

Jonathan's answer was a long pause that Daniel himself interrupted.

"Let me rephrase the question to make it easier for you to answer. Are you leaving me for her?"

"Look, Daniel…"

"Are you?"

"I don't know. It's not like that."

"What's it like then?"

"Not what you think."

"I'm thinking nothing at all. I'm completely without prejudice or precedents. I'm just hearing it for the first time, remember?"

"Your imagination is running wild," Jonathan said calmly.

"Well, perhaps that's so. So why don't *you* tell *me*."

"I don't know," was all he could come up with after a long pause.

"You don't know? Well, *I* know," Daniel said. "And I know that you're not leaving me without a fight. Face-to-face. Hand-to-hand combat, baby. So you'd better get working on those weights you've been neglecting—fast. Because you're going to be needing all the strength you can muster up by nightfall."

"What are you talking about?"

"I'm talking about how I'm going to come shit in your little love nest."

"You're crazy. You'd leave London, the film, the BBC?"

"The film? Fuck the film. How important can a film be when I have the opportunity to play Bette Davis and Clint Eastwood all in one in my own little drama?"

He was raving now, getting out of hand.

"Dan, you're upset."

"You'd better believe it."

"You'll feel better in the morning," Jonathan said.

"It *is* the morning here. A damp, dirty, rainy morning. I've been awake all night over you, wondering what terrible thing I've done to make you so testy, so unhappy, and now you sock me the news that I have some adolescent cooze for a replacement, and *I'm* the one that's crazy? The solitude must have gotten to you, just as I thought it would. You're acting like three-quarters of the fag-psycho ward at Payne-Whitney. Get her out of the house by the time I arrive or I swear, I'll put her through the blender, limb by limb!"

Jonathan was so startled by the line of attack, he almost laughed.

"I think you're jealous," he said.

Daniel ignored it. "Let's get off the phone so I can start calling British Airways."

"Don't be silly. You can't come here."

"Why not? It's half my house too. I paid the entire down payment, if you'll recall."

"Be rational, Daniel. You'll be fired from the film, word will get out immediately. You'll be called irresponsible. You'll be sued for endangering production. You'll never get work again. Your career will be washed up, now, at the very moment when it's finally going somewhere."

Calmly, "You're right. All the more reason to make her into purée of teenager and to beat the shit out of you when I get there. 'Bye."

"I don't believe you. You're acting like a Forty-second Street Puerto Rican transvestite."

"What are you acting like? Cary Grant? For chrissakes, Jonathan, you're obviously completely flipped out and need help desperately. I'll tell the producer you've gone bonkers. Everyone understands that."

Jonathan was no longer amused. "Well, do whatever you want to. Come here or stay there. I don't care. But know this: I'm not flipped out. The solitude hasn't gotten to me. I'm not schizoid from too much creative work. I'm quite sane, Daniel. And you're going to have to accept this as a sane decision. And it has nothing to do with getting some kind of twisted revenge on you, if that's what you're thinking."

"I don't think it's that at all," Daniel said.

"Good. Because it isn't. I don't know what it is really either. But I'm developing as a composer. And I've got to expand, to see things in other ways, to experiment. You're the one who always says, 'Change or Die.' Well, maybe that's what's happening to me. Maybe being gay *is* just a stage in one's development, as Freud thought. Or maybe we're capable of loving men and women equally well, equally validly. I've done a lot of thinking about this, Dan. You can't deny me the chance to change my life, can you? What right do you have to deny it? You're the one who always says 'Your first responsibility is to yourself.' God knows, you follow that philosophy. So, that's what I'm doing now, finding out what those responsibilities really are. What I really want. Who I really am. What my true commitments are."

It was a mouthful, Jonathan knew, sorry he'd gotten going on it. But after all, Daniel wanted it. It was clear he wouldn't settle for anything less. Yet Jonathan wondered where it had all come from. He certainly hadn't been thinking anything of the sort lately. He'd done everything possible to avoid thinking about it. Yet here it came forth, like some revivalist communicant spouting gibberish, talking in tongues. And its coming so made it seem all the more valuable now that it was said, as though unconsciously he'd been thinking this way all the while and was only now admitting it—to Daniel and to himself.

All the more surprise then when Daniel said, "I'll tell you who you are, Jonathan Lash. You're my lover of the past eight years. The person I love most in this love-filled and hate-filled existence. You are a brilliant, famous, still rising composer of popular music that may come to be regarded as classical in the not too distant future. You are someone who doesn't always know who or what precisely he wants. You are committed to music, the theater, the good life, great sex, and me—not necessarily in that order. That's who you are," Daniel concluded.

"As for what you are doing with that poor teenage girl, I can even sort of understand that, odd as it is. You're having what's known as a midlife crisis. Male menopause is another name for it. Everyone seems to be getting it lately. It means that all of a sudden you turn around and more than half your life is lived, and there's a great deal you haven't done you were certain you'd get a chance to do. All those boys you haven't slept with, all those books you haven't read, all those movies you just kept missing, all those pieces of music you intended to write but could never find the time for, all those wonderful places around the world you wanted to go to, but somehow never bought the tickets for when you had a free week. You turn around and see the present, and it is reality, which is the most hideous bringdown when you're creative and have wishes and whims. Reality, darling, r-e-a-l-i-t-y. Sorry, love. But that's what it is. And it's a drag, because you don't think it will alter, as it probably will, so subtly you'll be surprised, or so suddenly you'll go into shock. So you think, 'Man, this is it. Let me out.' I know, Jonathan. I went through the same changes last year myself. Remember? When I came home from Toronto and began playing around with the cute but dumb thing from the West Coast? You helped me through it then—good lover that you are, and you are the best—and now I'm going to help you through yours. See you tomorrow night. And get her out of the house!"

The phone clicked off.

Jonathan held it, dead, for a minute. He was blown away by Daniel's last barrage. Then he realized he still held the receiver.

He put it carefully in its cradle. Carefully, because suddenly everything around him seemed terribly fragile and frangible. The room he sat in—the so familiar room—looked totally alien, as though some subtle shift had altered its proportions since he'd been on the telephone: nothing he could measure, but clear, there.

His next reaction was disbelief—in the room, the house, the phone call, Daniel, himself. He even gripped the sides of the chair he sat in, as though he were in the middle of an earth tremor and the floor was about to give way.

That lasted a minute or so, and was followed by a slow but welling rise of rage at Daniel, which became intense, flashing anger, the kind that would make him explode.

When he calmed down a bit, he called the international operator and asked to have a call put through to Daniel's number. He was proud of how calmly he did this, how calmly he rehearsed to himself what he would say to Daniel, as the operator disappeared to find a line for him.

When she returned, she said he would have to wait for another line, perhaps twenty minutes.

He tried sitting there in the chair, waiting. But the words kept going around in his head, making him angry again, which he didn't want. So he stood up, went to the closet, found the pair of corduroy pants he'd given Stevie to wear the night of the storm, put them on, a little tight, and found a pair of sneakers and sweatshirt, put them on too, and went outside.

The beach was wide—low tide, he supposed—farther out than he'd seen it in weeks. Dancing algae were phosphorescent on the distant surf. The beach was heavy with damp, thick sand, almost as soft as silt. As though by night it had a second, different life; not the dry, gritty, individualized granular identity of daytime sand at all. The air was chilly, as he'd thought, but somehow warmer at the edge of the surf. A thin mist hung over it, to the horizon, separating the surging blackness of it from the moving, more evenly hued flatness of the starry night. No moon. It was too early for it to have already set. It must be up there somewhere—disguised in shadow: a new moon. Moon of beginnings, of late sowing, of pruning to encourage growth. Wasn't that how the Farmer's Almanac characterized the late September lunation?

Suddenly the energy damned up within him needed release. He jumped up, spread his arms and legs as far as he could, threw back his head, and yelled, letting the sound bellow out of him. Then, somewhat satisfied, he began to jog along the water's edge.

He ran the length of the community, thinking of nothing but how his arms and legs were moving, how the air was coming at him, how he was taking it in and exhaling it, how the sand beneath him was sometimes flat, angled down to the water, sometimes hard packed, damp, sometimes flooded by an errant wave. The breeze buffeted him, chilling every bead of perspiration that erupted on his face.

The run worked. When he returned to the house to dial again, he was exhausted, but considerably calmer: really calm, not like before.

Good thing too. For the international operator couldn't connect him to Daniel, and when he called Dan's office at the BBC productions, the switchboard operator told him she'd just received a call herself from Dan saying that he was going away for a holiday, and would return in a day or two.

Jonathan fumed at the news. What cheek!

What was he going to do now? Sleep would probably be impossible. But losing sleep because of Daniel was intolerable. So he went into the kitchen, heated up some milk, added a jigger, then another jigger of rum to it, and slogged it down.

Peeking into the bedroom, he saw that Stevie had fallen asleep. He hoped while they were still on the phone. Unusual for her, she wasn't all over the bed, but flat on her back, her breathing soft and regular.

He tried lying down in bed next to her, and trying to match the rhythm of his breathing to hers. No way. After a few minutes, all he could think of was Daniel, flying from London over this. This?

He got dressed again and went back out into the living area. He picked up a magazine, the book he'd been reading, his composing. All to no distractive effect at all.

Instead, he thought of an earlier phone call, this afternoon, while Stevie had been out on her errand to the post office: a call as upsetting now to Jonathan as it had been surprising and even amusing earlier.

He'd been at the piano, working on a trio between Don Farnace, Gentile, and Fiammetta in the last act. It was a tricky piece, with three separate related melodies that melded finally in a triple fugue. He'd promised himself he wouldn't answer the telephone if it rang. But when it did ring, he was so involved in his score he forgot that promise to himself. He immediately, impulsively picked it up, thinking it was Stevie calling to tell him the postmistress wouldn't give her his mail or with some other complication.

So, he'd answered the phone with alacrity, brightly said "Hello," accenting the second syllable.

He'd been greeted by silence, then a woman's voice that was neither Stevie nor the postmistress, asking if he were Jonathan Lash. His first thought was that it was Lady Bracknell, and he'd answered cautiously, hesitantly, "Yes. Yes it is."

"Good!" The voice seemed more businesslike; and now he was sure it wasn't Paula Locke: her voice was far more nasal. "I'm calling about a mutual friend, Stephanie Locke."

"She isn't here now," he said, then quickly amended that to, "I mean, I can pass on a message to her, but she isn't at home right now. Would you care to leave your name?"

"I will," his caller said, "if you promise not to say I called. I'm Rose Heywood."

"Oh!" he said involuntarily, possibly even with a sigh of relief. This was no enemy as Paula Locke would assuredly be, but a friend—Stevie's friend.

"And I really have to admit I'm pleased Stevie isn't there," Rose added. "I'd like to keep this chat between us, if that's all right with you, Mr. Lash."

Mysterious. But why not? he thought. "Sure."

"Good! You are amenable. I see this is going to be less difficult than I'd feared," Rose said. "My call concerns Stevie."

"Yes?"

"Well, actually Stevie and yourself. If you must know, I ordinarily detest people who go about interfering in others' lives. But then, sometimes one has no other choice, does one?"

"It depends."

"I mean, if *you* know the score and *I* know the score, but Stevie doesn't, well, then, I feel sort of duty bound to…" She faltered.

Jonathan tried to help her: "To let Stevie know the score too?"

"Yes! Well, no. Not exactly. She obviously knows the score too, or I wouldn't. But I wonder does she *really* know it?"

Jonathan hadn't an idea of what Rose was talking about. "You aren't referring to a specific score, a musical score, are you?"

"No. Why would I? Oh, that's right, isn't it? You're a composer. What an unfortunate choice of a word then. What I mean, Mr. Lash, is that…well, you've got to let Stevie go before she begins to get serious about you. Playing around, even flirting is fine, and I can understand your interest in Stevie. But you've got to end it all before something happens. Before she manages to trip you into the sack or something awful like that."

Jonathan paused. He really did find Rose delightful, no matter how interfering she was. He loved the way she said things, and used her last sentence back at her. "She already has tripped me into the sack."

"Oh, dear! I'm too late!" Rose said.

"Don't worry. Stevie uses the rhythm method of contraception. She'll be all right," he reassured her.

"It's not that, Mr. Lash. Stevie is confused right now. She's terribly impressionable, terribly imaginative."

"So am I," he said. "That's why we're…" He tried a few words, and ended up, "in the sack together."

A gloomy, "Right! I see!" from Rose. "That's what I inferred. But you must tell me, your intentions are honorable, aren't they?"

It was so old-fashioned he had to laugh. "I have no intentions."

"Toward Stevie?"

"Or if I do, that's for Stevie and me to discuss."

A pause. "I am interfering? I am out of place?" Rose asked, chastened.

"I'm afraid so."

"Well, I'm sorry about that. But I do care for her. And I don't want to see her hurt."

"Neither do I."

"And well, knowing what I do about you—after all, she had to tell someone, poor dear; every woman absolutely requires a confidante in these matters. But I want you to know I don't at all condone it."

"Did Stevie ask you to?"

"Well, not exactly. I mean, in a way."

"Look, Miss Heywood, I appreciate your concern. But we aren't really getting anywhere, and I'm working right now."

"I'm sorry about that," Rose said in a smaller voice. Then, more forcefully, "But I couldn't know about you two and just let it pass. She *is* young, and she *is* vulnerable, especially vulnerable right now. I suppose none of us wants to see the young go through difficulties the way we had to. Even though we know they must anyway."

"Stevie can take care of herself," Jonathan said. "I'll attest to that. Now, if you'll excuse me…"

"You won't tell her I called, will you?"

"No."

"All right. I'll let you go back to work. But tell me something, is it true that you're thirty-six years old?"

Jonathan was surprised by that question. "Yes."

"You sound a great deal younger," she concluded. "Good-bye."

Jonathan had put the receiver back in its cradle, had returned to the complicated trio and fugue, and had gotten back to work immediately, the odd phone call instantly banished from his thoughts.

Only to arise again later, during dinner with Stevie, by candlelight on the back deck; a dinner perfect but for the memory of the call, which cast a slight pall over it.

Now, Jonathan realized he'd been reacting to Rose Heywood's phone call and its unsubtle pressures, as well as to Dan when he'd called just now from London.

What *were* his intentions toward Stevie? Was this just a summer affair, a post–Labor Day sexfest? What intentions had he ever held toward her? Did he expect her to return to school, to see her only on weekends and holidays? Would he ask her to not return to school, to set up an apartment with him? To marry him? Could all that happen now, so late in his life? Of course it could, it had happened to others. And it wasn't too late. Dan himself was the baby of seven other siblings, he'd been sired when his father was over forty years old, his mother almost forty. Could Jonathan too begin a new life, and if so, what would that life be like with a wife? There would be children, of course; he couldn't see Stevie married without children. Schools, colleges, health care, the inexorable move to a larger apartment, even to a house, possibly out of Manhattan, for the kids' sake. There would be no longer a shared income—or at least if there were, it was unlikely that it would be as large as his and Dan's. Then too, he and Dan had over the years supported each other at different times: before *Little Rock* was a hit, when Dan was between jobs; in the doldrums last summer, before the BBC series came through. And they'd achieved a good financial balance since then. Married to Stevie, there would be new financial pressures on Jonathan. *Lady and the Falcon* would have to be a hit, a huge hit, one that gave birth to productions in London, Los Angeles; road shows, a movie sale. And the next show too, and the one after that...

I'll get no sleep tonight, he thought. That's some recompense to you, Dan, for your own sleepless night over me. If you really did have one. Which I only half believe anyway.

It would be just like Dan to lie about that. Idiot. And that ridiculous business about change of life. It really did sound as though they were all just housewives sitting around the laundry room, talking about their skin rashes and hemorrhoid conditions. Not to mention that incredible snow job about how he was coming to save him. What movie had Daniel seen to inspire that? Probably some screwball comedy from the thirties, where after this-ing and that-ing for three reels, the hero—say Jimmy Stewart—comes to his senses, and returns home to the girl who almost got away. Idiot! Dan's entire life seemed to derive from movies or shows. Hadn't Janet, his ex-wife, once confessed to Jonathan, "I didn't mind playing Margo Channing to his Max, but I did mind playing Robert Stack to his Marilyn Monroe in *Niagara*!" That summed it up. Poor Janet! What she'd had to put up with: and how few shared references she had to go by, in dealing with Dan. It must have been like living with the television tuned in to the Late Show all the time. Not that Dan had settled down much with Jonathan. Hardly. The time they got a black cleaning boy, and when the boy broke a lovely vase and began to apologize to Dan, what had Dan said? Of course he'd begun his Butterfly McQueen imitation: "I don't know *nothin'* about birthin' babies, Miss Scarlett!" he'd cried in the boy's face. Jonathan had a moment then when he was certain Dan was going to be the victim of a race riot in his very own living room. But no!

Dan, ever lucky. The boy had laughed, laughed uproariously. After that, he and Dan did *Amos 'n' Andy* routines whenever Jonathan was about. Idiot! Who did Dan think he was? His entire life was one scene after another—if not real, then certainly manufactured—one great moment after another: comic, tragic, pathetic, reflective—and often some indescribable mixture of them. What was he planning this time? Some mad rescue from across the sea? Some *Guns of Navarone* scenario, with Jonathan as the victim, the treasure, the secret document all rolled into one to be spirited away by SST to London? Or was Dan really simply bored over there, in need of a companion: someone to listen to his jibes, to remark on his accents, his witticisms at the expense of the place and the natives; someone to play straight man to him, to be the living audience to his living theater? Really, that's what it came down to: Dan didn't need a lover, he needed an audience!

His know-it-all attitude was especially galling, coming from someone who could barely take a cab across town without having some kind of mishap. "Just a change of life, darling. Male menopause, some call it. I had mine last year, remember?" That must be the role he'd decided on—he had to have a role—the friendly psychiatrist. He'd listen wonderfully, suffer patiently, even explain in detail what precisely it was that Jonathan was feeling, *as* he was feeling it. Dan's sympathy would be boundless, his attentiveness minutely calculated, his understanding complete and unremitting—unendurable. Jonathan would become the patient, the convalescent, Mr. Rochester after the house had burned down. It would be intolerable!

"...a teenager." She wasn't really a teenager at all. In many ways, Stevie was far more mature than Dan would be at seventy...

"...that's who you are!" Said so smugly, Jonathan could have slapped him for it. The whole speech, in fact, cried out to be completed by a hefty backhand across Dan's complacent mug. Especially that "in this love-filled and hate-filled existence" touch! Leave it to Dan to embroider so cunningly, so spontaneously, one scarcely noticed the embroidery it was—unless you knew him as well as Jonathan did. He was probably already mentally fitting on his Dr. Kildare jacket as he said the words, gazing admiringly at his own compassionately fixed face in the mirror.

"I *do* have a right to change, to be myself," Jonathan said aloud, but softly, so as not to wake Stevie. "I'll take the chances. I'll take the responsibility. Wherever it may lead."

And so on, and so forth, until morning.

CHAPTER SIXTEEN

S tevie's first hint that all was not well was that Jonathan was not in bed next to her when she awakened. Of course, there was always the off chance that he'd gotten up early. He'd done that before.

She threw on the T-shirt and shorts dropped by the bed last night, and went out into the living area. No Jonathan. He might be at the beach.

Brewing coffee, she realized how effortlessly she now went through all the preparations she'd had to think about a week ago: grinding the beans, selecting the mixture, boiling cold tap water only to the first whistle of the kettle, pouring just enough of the water into the filtered cone so that it merely dampened the ground coffee, letting that seep, then pouring the rest of the water in slowly. She knew she'd never make instant coffee again—or if so, only in an emergency. It wasn't the technique of the coffee-making she'd accepted, so much as the evident higher quality of the result— coffees that leapt at you, that caressed the palate, that were desserts, experiences. The gap that had suddenly yawned open between her and that man—Matt—that's what that had been all about: her commitment to quality, to the better things in life. Of course there had been other matters involved too—almost too many of them for her to think about. But that point stood out; how first through Rose Heywood, and now through Jonathan she'd learned to aim a little higher in life—higher than her parents had ever thought to teach her, despite their devotion to money and what it could buy. She hoped Jonathan would be back soon, before she had to reheat the coffee and ruin its flavor.

The second sign that this was not going to be a good day happened when she looked out the kitchen door. For the first time in weeks, there was no sun. Instead there was a warm, yellowish mist that seemed to hang inches away—so that when she stepped out onto the deck, coffee mug in hand, her skin was immediately clammy. It wasn't thick—nothing like a real fog—and it might still burn off before noon. But it seemed all-pervasive. It beaded the lawn furniture, strung droplets on spiderwebs, covered the bushes with a heavier dew than usual, darkened the wood decks in splotches of dampness, hid the surf from view.

It was bound to happen. Two weeks of perfectly sunny, clear weather had to break sometime, she told herself. But why today?

Walking around the house, she encountered the third sign portending trouble: asleep on a brown and white plastic chaise longue, his clothing soaked through, his face shining with dew, the hood of his sweatshirt pulled up around his face like a visor— Jonathan.

She looked at him for a minute, deciding whether to wake him or not. She decided she had to—if only because of the dampness; it might lead to a chill, to a cold, to who knew what.

He looked so exhausted, even asleep. His face seemed fragile, and oddly pale, despite his rich tan. His body, too, seemed contorted, so unlike the ease with which he ordinarily took his rest. One hand was twisted inside his sweatshirt, the other curled around and inside a pocket of the shirt. One leg dangled off the chaise completely, the other leg was half under it. He reminded her of Grünewald's painting of the Crucifixion she'd studied in school, where the foreground Christ just removed from the cross was contorted like this; each bend of a finger, each jutting elbow or bony knee gave an emotional charge to what otherwise was a rather static depiction.

"Jonathan," she whispered, touching his face with a finger.

It was enough. His eyes opened. They didn't immediately focus on her.

"You fell asleep," she said. "You're wet. You ought to change."

He sat up and looked around. He made a face at the weather as though to say, "I told you so," although he didn't say anything.

"I made fresh coffee." She offered her mug to him.

When he didn't take it, she said, "I don't know how long you've been out here. But I think you ought to take a hot shower and change into dry clothing."

He sighed loudly, forcefully. "Morning," he said, then reached up to her. His kiss on her cheek was clammy and brief. He got up and went into the house.

She followed a few minutes later, after telling herself she was being foolish. So what if it was a lousy day. They'd stay inside, listening to music, perhaps; sitting by a blazing fire; doing what they usually did. It might be pleasant for a change if it grew stormy and rained hard. He'd awaken, get warm, and be himself. He couldn't be comfortable in that position for hours, out here in the dampness. She made a cup of coffee the way she knew he liked it and brought it into the big bathroom.

He was just getting out of the shower. He took the coffee, sipped it, wrapped himself in a large Egyptian motif towel, and sat down on the toilet seat, avoiding her look.

Stevie felt so suddenly, utterly distant from him, she had to do something for contact. She picked up a smaller towel and began toweling his hair in soft little massaging motions.

"You have wonderful hair," she said.

"What's left of it."

"There's plenty. Only this." She lightly tapped the bald spot in the center back of his skull. "You can hide that easily. It's hidden most of the time anyway, because your hair is so curly."

"I've been covering it for five years. Good coffee."

"I hope you don't come down with something."

"I feel all right. It was warm out."

"But damp. Were you out there long?"

"An hour or two."

"Couldn't sleep?"

"No."

"Did you fight with Dan?"

"Didn't have the chance to fight with him."

"Maybe that's better," she said. It was one of the most direct conversations they'd had; but it was necessary, she felt, for it to be so. "There! That's pretty well dry." She moved around in front of him, and began to rub the big towel over his chest, then opened up the towel, and began drying him with another smaller drier towel.

"You don't have to do this," he said.

"Try to stop me."

When she'd reached the area of his groin, he lifted her face and put his own down next to it. For a second she thought they were going to kiss—but no. He simply looked at her. He seemed sad, resigned, very handsome and quiet.

"I have to go into the city today."

When she didn't answer, but continued to allow her face to be held, and continued to stare at him, he said: "Dan's coming here."

She lowered her eyes then, knowing that what she saw in his eyes was pain; she couldn't stand looking at him, knowing that's what it was.

"I don't know what's going to happen," he said.

She pulled out of his loose hold on her, and sat back on her haunches, her eyes still averted.

"I don't know if I'm saying this well. You're the first woman I've ever been this close to, and you're so different from a man."

She looked up and even smiled a little. He was so unhappy.

"I mean, I'm not sure how to gauge what you're thinking, what you're feeling as I talk. You seem so…" He appeared to give up. "I don't know. So different."

"Vive la difference," she said, trying to make it into a joke.

Then he did kiss her. Softly, warmly, but briefly. He pulled back before she could respond.

"He's flying in today. Coming out here, he said. He wants some kind of confrontation. Which is fine with me. But I don't want you around."

Now she saw a trace of anger replace the pain and sadness in his eyes; and now she really began to feel afraid for them, for him, for herself. She threw her arms around his waist, her head into his lap, and held him tightly, as though if only she could keep holding him tightly now, all would be well.

"I don't know when I'll be back here," he said. "Maybe... maybe, you ought to close up your family's place too."

"And then?" she mumbled. She wasn't sure she wanted even to know.

"I don't know."

So here it was, Stevie thought. I'm holding him, but he's already gone. Tears came to her eyes as though it was already over, to be mourned for. But she wouldn't let them fall, wouldn't let this happen. She would change this moment, as she had changed yesterday's incident with Matt. This too was a test of some sort for her. Something for her to pass through, not fall into, if she were to go on. She had to show who she was—who, potentially, at least, she could be.

She wiped her eyes on his towel-covered legs, and looked up.

"All right," she said, pleased by the steady tone of her voice. "We'll close up and go into town together." She even managed a smile. "No sense hanging around here if it's going to be nasty weather, is there?"

His steady look was unfathomable.

She stood up, rather than fall victim again to her worst fears. "Come on. Stand up," she said. "Let me dry you off properly."

He let her, and that pleased her. Once more she was able to see, touch, and review this body, once more be thrilled and astonished by how perfectly he fitted into that heretofore unsuspected ideal she had unconsciously earlier formed of what the right man for her would look like.

For a minute, she thought they might make love, he seemed so comfortable in her hands. But he never got erect; only kissed her and played with her breasts a little, before shrugging. She let it pass. He had things on his mind.

They spent the next few hours having a leisurely breakfast and then packing for the trip to the city.

The sun came out briefly around noon, bringing up the temperature to an uncomfortable damp warmth, but it never completely burned off the mist. By the time the two houses were deemed ready, the sun was gone, and a sickly yellow green mist had replaced the earlier yellow gray one. At sunset it would turn a gray green. It would be an eerie night out here. She was almost glad she would miss it.

After a phone call, Jonathan discovered there would be no seaplanes flying because of the bad weather. Visibility was too low.

His attempts to get them a limousine on the other side of the bay were tiring and fruitless, despite his calling three cab services. They'd have to ferry across and take a train into the city.

Their walk to the harbor was silent, both of them oppressed by the weather and the almost alien shapes the familiar landscape evoked with the sudden coming and going of the heavy mist.

Closer to the bay, the mist seemed almost fog. It was white, however, rather than that awful color. The ferryboat they rode across the bay was one she'd never been on before: small, closed-in, small-windowed, musty, as though seldom used—although Jonathan said it was the usual off-season boat. It was the last ferry; the boat schedule had been reduced to four crossings a day. She and Jonathan sat in the back section, surrounded by luggage, most of it his. The front of the boat was occupied by haggard-looking workers returning to the shore side: construction men, carpenters, plumbers, a few clerks from the two stores still open on the island. From behind, one of them looked like Matt. But of course, Stevie reminded herself, Matt was a ferry hauler himself; he would ride across on one of the flatboats he'd loaded and unloaded.

Jonathan was, if not in good spirits, at least not as grim as when she'd awakened him. He'd taken two large leather valises in addition to the flight bag slung across his shoulder, saying that now was as good a time as any to start moving stuff back to town. He sat back among them in the corner of the boat, reading a book on Italian art. She kept her hand in one of his, in his lap. Sometimes he held it. Sometimes he would let go of it, to turn a page, and forget to take it back again.

The shore side of the ferry station—ordinarily a bustling scene of people, cars, trucks, and shops—was as desolate as the island side.

The railroad station, a half green lean-to, its paint much chipped and discolored by bad weather, surrounded by tall trees, was as lost in the fog, as mysterious to her as any depicted in a nineteenth-century Gothic novel. It was much cooler on shore than it had been on the island, where heat was retained by the mist and lack of breezes. They sat on the rickety built-in seat, along with two elderly ladies who occasionally stared at them. Once more Jonathan held her hand. They didn't speak. Both had put on windbreakers. Hers was bright blue, his a brilliant yellow.

The train that finally arrived was an express, but as it went in the wrong direction to attract many passengers during rush hour, it was initially deserted. They took a double-facing seat in the back of one car near the doors. Jonathan soon went to sleep against her shoulder. Stevie remained awake, checking outside the dirty green-tinted windows at the bleak and dreary passing scenery. She tried not to think about anything, and succeeded fairly well, but she couldn't bring herself to nap. She reminded herself that he'd only gotten an hour or two out on the deck after being awake all night.

At one stop, two young women came into the car, at the door nearest her. They seemed to be about her age, working girls, just on their way home. They stopped, and were turning to come into the section of the car where she and Jonathan were, then hesitated.

As they paused, Stevie could suddenly see herself and Jonathan as though she were one of the two girls. The older, handsome man sleeping against her shoulder: their casual clothing, obviously summer wear; their deep tans; the bags around them, on the seats and floor; his art book face down on the opposite seat. The girls' eyes rose to meet Stevie's and seemed to ask her: Is this true what we are seeing? Is he your lover? Are you just back from a vacation? Are you both wonderfully attractive and happy and terribly in love?

Stevie's look back to them was bold, confident. "Yes!" it said, "Yes. It's all true."

They turned around then, embarrassed or happy or upset—she

didn't know which or in what combination of the three—and went away toward another section of the car. They never looked back.

She exulted. Yes, she'd told them, without words, but told them clearly enough anyway. And, yes, they'd seen and believed, and left her, unwilling to invade the delicacy of her love bubble. She said yes because now, in their eyes, at this moment, if not forever, it was true. She loved and was loved, was happy and could make someone happy; she was strong, getting stronger all the time.

It followed her throughout the trip, would follow her for a long time to come, she suspected.

When the train next stopped and Jonathan shifted in his sleep, she slipped off his shoulder, kissed him lightly, on one cheek, and said so low that he couldn't hear her, "Thank you. Thank you for giving me this moment." He mumbled a bit, and she let him put his head in her lap, while she contemplated the various futures that lay in front of her—until the train went into a tunnel, and she knew they would be at Penn Station in Manhattan in a few minutes.

"Rest well?" she said, awakening Jonathan.

"Terrific. You make a great pillow."

"Thank mother nature," she said. "Built-in padding."

"I really needed that," he said, getting up, rubbing his eyes, looking out the windows at the blackness. Even though it wasn't a smoking car, he lighted a cigarette.

"Where are we?"

"Almost there," she said, gathering the bags together. The train pulled into the station a minute later. The platform was filled four deep with people who Stevie knew would be getting into this car, charging right by her, whether she was in or out.

It took them as long to stand up and organize the carrying of the bags as it did for the train to stop and the doors to open.

They managed to get out of the train and halfway through the crowd pressing to board. But as he was encumbered with more bags than she, she was out before him, at the empty side of the platform. So she was able to spot Daniel Halpirn among the stragglers trying to get into the next car.

He was back, as Jonathan said he would be. He was on his way to Sea Mist.

She couldn't let him get on, not after the long, tiring airplane trip across the Atlantic already today. He would take this long trip by train and wait for the ferry to the island and still not find Jonathan there. That would be too awful for him. For all of them. She couldn't let it happen.

Rushing, she stopped him by pulling his arm as he was stepping into the train.

He looked at her, without recognizing her; looked at her surprised, with irritation, as though to say, let go of me.

"Daniel!" she called into his ear, over the noise of the train and the loudspeakers and the people. "Don't get on!" She tugged at him again.

He looked back again, then recognized her.

"Stevie?"

She nodded, and continued pulling at his arm. They were in the middle of a new rush of people trying to board the train behind them. She had to hold on to the side of the car to keep upright.

"Where's Jonathan?" he asked her, having to shout it.

She nodded behind her. She could just make out Jonathan, stopped by a stairwell, looking around for her through the bobbing heads of the crowd.

"We came in," she said, and managed to pull Dan out of the doorway, to a spot where they wouldn't be buffeted by people.

Daniel looked confused.

"I was just going out."

"Don't have to now," she said. She felt embarrassed. He looked over her shoulder at where she knew Jonathan was standing. Daniel's face was tight, hard; he seemed very unsure of what to do, of what to say.

"Here," she said, handing him one of Jonathan's bags she'd been carrying.

Dan looked down at the bag, and recognizing it, took it, and slung it across his shoulder by the strap. But he was still confused.

"He's already carrying too many," she said.

He looked past her again, toward Jonathan, then back at her. The crowd was thinning out on the platform as people pressed to get into the train, rushing down the stairs.

"I don't understand," Daniel said to her.

She reached up to speak into his ear, and had to hold him by one shoulder to support herself, he was so tall. "Say good-bye to him, for me, will you," she said. "Say Stevie thanks him."

He stared at her.

"And please, don't fight with him," she said, "Please, don't do anything bad to him, anything to make him unhappy."

"Why are you doing this?" Daniel said, only half comprehending.

It was clear he would never do anything like it.

"Don't ask me," she said. "Just do it. And be happy." He kissed her cheek lightly now; she smelled a cologne that had steeped Jonathan's bedroom—as though Daniel were a tomcat who'd spread his scent everywhere on his territory. That persuaded her. She knew she was doing the right thing.

"Be happy," she repeated. "Don't fight with him."

"I won't! I won't. I promise," he said, and it was clear that he was overjoyed. "Good-bye. Good-bye. Thank you. Thank you."

"Good-bye," she said, and now her decision made, final, the tears she'd held back this morning started up again in her eyes. She turned away from the train and Daniel and walked away quickly, her vision slightly blurred, until she reached up and wiped her face.

Last-minute commuters raced down the stairs past her as she slowly ascended the steps.

At the top of the stairs, she turned around and looked back. Only a few latecomers were dashing madly into the cars. In the distance, by the next stairway, stood two figures with bags at their feet, staring at each other, not speaking, not touching.

"Good-bye," she said. "Good-bye, lovers!" she said, finally. Then turned and went into the station to find a telephone and a taxicab.

CHAPTER SEVENTEEN

Daniel was waiting for him in the Martinson's coffee shop as he said he would be. He was sitting in a booth, facing out toward the station, a mostly empty cup of coffee on the table; he was reading *Variety,* intensely interested in some item. He looked so normal, in such an expected attitude, that for a moment Jonathan's anger at him diminished. Vulnerable, he went and sat down. Daniel folded the paper and put it next to his seat, to give Jonathan his full attention. The expression on his face was unclear to Jonathan, who wasn't certain he could trust it anyway.

"Any luck?" Dan asked.

So that was the tack he was going to take—the innocent bystander. Two could play that.

"I can't find her anywhere," Jonathan said. "What precisely did she say to you?"

"I told you before. There was so much noise down on the platform and it all happened so fast."

"What were her words?" Jonathan insisted.

Dan didn't waver. "She handed me your flight bag and wished me good luck or something. I thought she was talking about the films with the BBC. I wasn't even sure who she was for a minute."

Jonathan didn't believe that. "Really?"

"I certainly wasn't expecting to meet *her.* Or you either. I was on my way to beard you in your lair, remember?"

"And that's all she said?"

"That's all," Dan said, relieved. Then, "No. Wait a minute. Of course that wasn't all. She said to say good-bye to you."

That was the key point. Jonathan's entire body—stimulated into action looking for her the last three-quarters of an hour—suddenly sagged back, exhausted, into the booth.

"Just that? 'Good-bye'?"

"No. 'Good-bye, have a good life,' or something like that. I'm afraid that's what she said." Dan's face was a mask of sympathy and sincerity—feigned sincerity, Jonathan thought.

"Not call me later, or anything like that?"

"Why don't you call her? If she left right after I saw her, she ought to be at home by now."

"I couldn't get her phone number. There were a dozen Lockes listed. None of the names seemed familiar. What is his name? Lord Bracknell?"

"Got me. Clifton? Paul?"

"No. That's Lady Bracknell. Paula. No Paula Locke listed either."

"Maybe we have it in the phone book at home," Dan suggested. "We ought to have it somewhere, no? They're our neighbors. What if their place went on fire at Sea Mist or something. I'm sure we can find it."

Dan was right. Someone they knew must have the Lockes' city home number. He'd get it and call Stevie and... What if Dan were telling the truth about her, though? What if she'd said what he told Jonathan, what if she had given him the flight bag and told him to relay her good-bye? Would she repeat that on the phone when he finally got through? Of course she would. Far more awkwardly. What could have prompted the sudden change? Seeing Dan at the station?

He looked at Dan, who was surreptitiously glancing down at *Variety* on the seat next to him.

"It's some deal the two of you worked up," Jonathan suddenly said, and as suddenly believed it.

"Me and your teenager?" Dan seemed amused. "When? When did we have the chance to?"

"I don't know when." Jonathan cast his thoughts back. Hadn't she awakened him for Dan's call last night? They could have talked then.

"What about when she picked up the phone?"

"Last night?" Dan said, sincerity galore.

Now Jonathan was convinced of it. "Sure, last night. I can just hear you two. I can hear you operating on her, she'd be half asleep, half frightened of you anyway."

Dan lifted his coffee cup and tossed down the dregs grandly. "Do you think I actually *expected* to find some girl answering our phone? All but six words we exchanged were an attempt to establish the fact that I hadn't reached a wrong number." He stood up. "Want a coffee? It clears up muddy thinking, you know."

Jonathan felt defeated by Dan's reasoning, which made far more sense than his own rather foolish accusation. Of course that must have happened. At first. But that still didn't mean Dan hadn't the opportunity to browbeat Stevie. Unless she got away as fast as she realized who was calling? Which made sense too.

"Well?" Dan asked. "Coffee?"

Jonathan looked around at the plastic tables and sordid customers. He didn't want to be here. He didn't want to be having this conversation either.

"Let's go."

When they had ascended to the street, Jonathan felt the oppressive warmth and incredible humidity. The air was so thick and heavy you could reach out and grab it—grab it, that is, if you wanted to get dirty, oily. Every car or bus that passed them on Eighth Avenue sent out exhaust fumes that were instantly assimilated into the already semigelatinous air, making him gag. This same weather had been a yellow fog at Sea Mist, so cool he and Stevie had to put on windbreakers at the train station only a few hours ago. It seemed so long ago, suddenly. In such another place.

Dan found them an air-conditioned cab and they rode in

silence up to their apartment. Passersby seemed stunned by the heat, moving slowly, purposelessly, as though they were zombies. At the end of the ride, the cabbie and Dan spoke about the heat wave that had uncharacteristically struck the city in late September. For the first time since he'd returned, Dan's speech had all of the British inflection Jonathan had heard increasingly in their telephone conversations. Even the driver thought so. When they got out and Dan paid him, the cabbie asked if they were Australian.

The apartment looked small—of course it would, after being in the outdoors for months, with the ocean and the bay's seven miles to the horizon on either side, as the real walls to life in Sea Mist. Big as the apartment was, it seemed small, dark, oppressive.

Dan immediately went around turning on the air-conditioning outlets in each room; their soft humming filled up the place. Jonathan looked up the Lockes' phone number in their address book, but only found the one for their Sea Mist home listed. He felt defeated again. He flipped the pages of the address book, hopping from page to page, trying to remember the names of some of their other neighbors. All he could recall was their former neighbor, Cass, who recently sold her house to a South American couple who had visited it once in July.

Dan was back in the living room by the time Jonathan had begun to dial.

"Why don't you try the Sea Mist fire department? They must have all the residents' phone numbers, no?"

Jonathan followed that suggestion. But he reached a recording that only gave him an emergency number. No one was at the fire house. It was a volunteer unit anyway, drawn by an elaborate fire alarm system in the community. Another little defeat. So, he dialed the police station, which also gave him an emergency number, plus the phone number of the main police force station on the mainland. No sense trying them.

It was dark outside when he tried to reach Cass for the third time without any success. Daniel was in the kitchen when Jonathan finally hung up the phone. He must have been talking to someone in London—his producer at the BBC. Daniel was being calm, firm, vaguely explanatory.

"What do we have to eat?" Jonathan brushed past where Dan sat astride a tall stool.

Dan said "Ta" and hung up. "Nothing, unless you can whip something gourmet out of ketchup, a box of poppers, and dead tonic water."

Jonathan closed the refrigerator door. As he walked out of the kitchen, Dan spun on the stool and grabbed him around the waist. "Hey, babe, I'm sorry."

Jonathan flinched at Dan's touch, and Dan's arms fell away. Embarrassment hung in the room between them as though it were tangible. Jonathan felt the first pang of guilt since he'd met Dan at the train station. He broke the silence first. "What did they say in London?"

"Nothing." His advances rejected, Dan's voice sounded chastened. "I'm to take however much time is needed, they told me. But no more than three days, or they'll have my ass in court."

"Three days for what?" And, as Dan didn't answer, "You might as well go back tonight."

"I want to take you back with me," Dan said.

"What for? As proof that you aren't just taking a sudden temperamental vacation?"

"I don't need proof," Dan said, with an edge of impatience, the first sign of any kind of crack in his role so far. He must have noticed it too, because he stood up and went to the bar. "How about a drink?"

"The tonic water is flat."

"We'll drink it neat. We could both use one." He fixed them two vodkas and added ice cubes. They didn't look at each other as they sipped. The strong liquor coursed through Jonathan's chest and stomach. But it did calm him.

"So you're just going to hang around for three days?"

"I suppose."

"What do you hope to accomplish?"

"Do you really want to know?" Dan asked.

Jonathan wasn't completely certain he did want to know. "Sure," he said.

"You're expecting me to say that I'm staying here three days until you come to your senses, at which point, I'll sweep you away on the Concorde."

"Something like that," Jonathan admitted.

"Well, that's what I thought too, at first. But I see it's not going to work. It'll take longer before you come to your senses. You're a mess, Jonathan, a seething, confused, emotional mess."

"Thanks for the encouragement. I thought you were going to play Dr. Kildare, not the doctor in *The Snake Pit.*"

"The three days," Dan went on, ignoring that statement, "are to give you time enough to contact your little teenager and to get your act straightened out between the two of you. With that settled, I'll leave satisfied."

"Meaning what?"

"Meaning you get hold of her, and she confirms what she told me at Penn Station."

"Or she doesn't confirm it."

"Whatever," Dan said airily.

"And you want to wait around for that?" Jonathan asked. "Even if you are missing three days of shooting?"

"I wouldn't miss it for the world," Dan said smugly.

"You planned this. I don't know how. But you did."

"Wrong! For once, Jonathan, it's your show. I'm just the audience. Now let's be civilized and go have dinner somewhere. I'm starving what with all the suspense of boy meets girl, boys loses girl, and all that running around Penn Station."

It was as though Dan had struck his face, and thrown the glove down at Jonathan's feet.

"Don't be so sure of yourself," he warned, "or you may go back to London a very unhappy man."

"I'm unhappy now!"

"I'm going to take a shower," Jonathan announced. "The air here is like an oil slick."

In the shower, he turned on the massage nozzle to full blast and basked under its ministrations, letting it batter away the tension that knotted his neck and back. At one point, with his palms flat up against the tile wall he leaned against, he suddenly felt so released, he let out a grunt, a sigh, and what he thought might be a sob. He stifled it. But he knew he felt frustrated: angry at Dan, at Stevie, at himself. He turned around, dialed the massage for a softer setting, and rubbed his skin hard with the loofah.

Drying off, he had an idea. If he called the Lockes' number at Sea Mist, the operator there might be able to give him their Manhattan number. He wrapped a towel around himself, and went to the bedroom to try it.

"Certainly, sir," the operator said. "The number in Manhattan is…"

He couldn't believe his luck. He hung up, and dialed the number. Busy.

Buoyed up by this, he got dressed. When he reached Stevie, he would immediately ask her out to dinner, not discuss anything on the phone. She'd been upset when she saw Dan. Right now she was probably crying her eyes out for letting herself be bamboozled by him. Either that, or during the train trip, as he'd slept, she'd reached some absurd conclusion, and decided to nobly abandon him to Dan, à la Sidney Carton ascending the stairs to the guillotine in *A Tale of Two Cities*—"It's a far, far better thing than I have ever done…"

Dressed, Jonathan tried the number again. This time a machine answered: Mr. and Mrs. Vernon Locke. Of course, that was Lord Bracknell's name! No mention of Stevie on the tape. Did she have her own unlisted phone? Didn't most teenagers who still lived at home? He couldn't really leave a message on this line. What if she hadn't told her parents about him? Would she? If not, they might think he was calling about some emergency situation concerning their house in Sea Mist. Even worse, what if he did leave his name for Stevie, and she didn't answer? What if she were sitting by the machine right now, waiting for his call, a call she would never respond to? No. She must be out with her parents, reconciling. The busy signal before must have been another incoming call being answered by the machine. He would call back in an hour or two.

"Ready?" Jonathan asked brightly when he emerged from the bedroom. Half scowling, Dan led them out of the apartment.

They descended and had gone two blocks along Central Park West before Jonathan asked where they were going.

"Balzac's," Dan answered. "It's a new restaurant Ronnie and Dorian opened up on Columbus Avenue. I promised we'd drop in and try it out."

Jonathan hadn't even heard of Ronnie and Dorian before.

Balzac's was two large storefronts on the ground level with the walls between them taken down, revealing six large supporting pillars. Story-and-a-half glass windows fronted the street, with doors on either side. One of these led to a raised platform with a semicircular bar enclosing a waiting area. A balcony swept up along the longest side, the rear wall of the restaurant, covered with dark cloth and lucite-framed watercolors. Chrome railings ran along the balcony, up and down the pillars, around other built-in furniture, and all around the room in one form or another—accenting the industrial carpeting, subdued colors, and dark, practical fabrics. The tables were lacquered black, as were the small, dim lamps on the table. Even the bud vases—some holding an orchid, some a calla lily—were lacquered or burnished metal. Every touch attested that Balzac's was the very latest in what Dan called "haute fag" decor, which had begun in discos and tiny apartments years before, and had since swept the city. Because it was located on the Upper West Side, Balzac's clientele was more mixed than if it were in the Village. Still, it was mostly peopled tonight by young male couples in the Lacoste shirt, blue Levi's jeans outfit of the New York gay man. The waiters, though more casually dressed, seemed equally gay. The maître d' might have come right off the pages of the latest *Gentleman's Quarterly,* and must have at least been an unemployed actor. He checked Dan's reservation—made, Jonathan supposed, only a short while ago, when he was in the shower—pointed to the table on the balcony they would have, and asked them to wait in the lounge.

It was clear Dan chose Balzac's not because he'd promised the owners he'd come: Balzac's didn't seem to be lacking business. No, he'd done it, and gotten a table where they would be seen so Jonathan would behave himself, not throw a scene, under risk of social ostracism, or at least instant widespread gossip emanating from the half dozen acquaintances he'd nodded to since they'd entered. That was fine with Jonathan. He had no intention of arguing with Dan—here or anywhere else. But he was surprised by how little Dan trusted him tonight. Unless, of course, Dan knew he would come out the loser in any argument they had.

"My treat," Dan announced, as they were seated.

Jonathan sipped his vodka and perused the menu. Evidently the restaurant's name derived from the selection of courses offered—all French, although more on the level of the Brasserie than La Céte Basque.

The waiter was cute and perfectly built, this emphasized by the close-fitting chinos and T-shirt. Jonathan had seen so many of this type before in the city, he wondered if they were genetically manufactured somewhere in the Midwest, exclusively to be shipped at the age of twenty-one to New York to be waiters in smartly decorated restaurants. They were all so alike, so alert, efficient, indifferent. They took orders easily, remembered with ease long lists of daily altering special dishes of bewildering complexity. They even sometimes smiled at jokes. They almost seemed human.

"Believe me, there are few young men like that in London," Dan sighed after the waiter had taken their menus.

"Thank God," Jonathan said.

"I think he's adorable," Dan came back. "And so does everyone else in this place."

Jonathan contented himself with a "hmph." He wasn't going to get into an fight over the waiter.

"At least," Dan amended, "everyone in the room who isn't a temporarily demented pseudoheterosexual."

Jonathan let that pass, without even a "hmph." He looked over the room, inspecting faces. Most of those familiar to him had gone.

The appetizers arrived, and with their pâtés and salads,

someone Jonathan vaguely recognized, who proved to be one of the owners, Dorian, a slightly aged, heavier and graying version of their waiter. He and Jonathan were reintroduced, and Dorian pulled a spare chair over for a few minutes of chitchat. Since Jonathan looked at the main floor most of the time, Dan had to do most of the chatting. Dorian was easily prodded into asking about London and the films he was directing, so this proved pleasant and gratifying to Dan. At one point, Jonathan, only half listening, thought he saw Stevie among a group of some six people looking in, inspecting the menu taped inside one huge window. He stared at the girl so long, so intently, even from this far away, that another party in the girl's group noticed him and pointed him out. When the girl turned, Jonathan saw she was heavier, older than Stevie. He looked back to the table, to Dan and Dorian.

"This pâté isn't half bad," Dan announced after Dorian left.

Jonathan spent most of the meal distracted. The entrée was eaten methodically, mechanically; he scarcely tasted it. He thought about seeing her again.

He might not reach her tonight. Even tomorrow. She might have gone back to school directly from Sea Mist.

Was that possible? There seemed so many possibilities for what had happened at the train station: at the same time so many possible reconciliations too. He began imagining them. She would call, say she'd been out of town, at school, and had just gotten back, just gotten his call, and she'd be right over. Or he'd pick up his mail downstairs tomorrow where all the residents' mailboxes were, and he would find a note hand-delivered from her, explaining the misunderstanding, asking him to contact her, or at least not making it seem as impossible, as final as that good-bye she'd supposedly asked Dan to tell him.

These fantasies soon devolved into coincidental meetings. They would encounter each other in the park some afternoon, by the little pond. She would be casual, shy. Their conversation would be tactful and delicate. She would calmly explain why she had left him at the train station. It would be something banal she'd had to do, something she'd already told him before they left Sea Mist if only he'd listened. He would then gently release the fact that Dan had gone back to London. They would kiss, walk through the park to his apartment—the leaves turning, spangled with sunlight like Japanese paper umbrellas. Upstairs, they would make love. She would cry for a minute. He would... His fantasies were broken by the waiter's sudden arrival with a message.

"A party in the restaurant who wishes to remain anonymous would like to buy you drinks. May I take your order?"

His words snapped Jonathan back into reality.

"Are you sure?" he asked.

The waiter was prepared. "Are you Mr. Lash?"

"Yes."

"Well, that's who the drinks are for," he said, rechecking the name on the tab.

Dan was looking out over the balcony; Jonathan supposed for the donor.

"It must be from Dorian," he concluded.

"It's not from the management," the waiter said. "Another waiter gave me the message."

As Jonathan continued to stare, Dan asked, "Well? How about brandies with our coffee?"

"Whatever," Jonathan agreed.

"Who do you know here who would send us drinks anonymously?" Jonathan asked.

"Send *you* drinks, you mean. I didn't see anyone. Maybe it's one of your fans. Poor thing, cowering behind a potted palm, so pleased to have caught a glimpse of you."

"Come off it," Jonathan said. He tried to lapse back into his thoughts about Stevie. Where had he been?

When the waiter brought coffee and the drinks, he asked Jonathan, "Are you a celebrity or something?"

Dan had to hold a napkin over his face to suppress his mirth.

The waiter became embarrassed and began to withdraw.

"I'm a porno star," Jonathan said on impulse. "Can't you tell?"

"Oh," he said tonelessly.

"Really, Jonathan," Dan said, "you *are* a bundle of surprises these days. First you're a latent hetero, then you have your claque following us, and now you're in fuck flicks. I thought I knew you inside out."

To avoid getting drawn into sparring with Dan, Jonathan excused himself from the table. He found a pay phone near the men's room, and dialed the Locke residence. The machine answered again. As he passed the waiter, the boy looked at him closely, trying to figure out who exactly he was.

"I'm *not* a porno star," Jonathan said.

"I didn't think you were."

He and Dan had no further words in the restaurant. Dan paid and they left.

"I guess you wouldn't want to stroll through the park?" Dan asked when they reached Central Park West.

Jonathan saw what interested him, a pay phone across the street, on the edge of the park. It was the same to him whether they went right home or walked. He tried the number again, and again was greeted by the taped message. Each time this happened, it seemed to drain energy from him; at the same time it prompted him to call yet again. He began to feel like one of the animal subjects of behavioral modification lab experiments.

He allowed Dan to lead them onto a path south from the Seventy-second Street entrance, past a score of men sitting on the wrought iron railings.

"Where are we going?" he asked.

"Don't worry. I'm not going to drag you into the Rambles and incite a gang rape so that you come to your senses. We're walking in the park. Nothing else."

A wind was soughing through the heavy foliage around them. Although it did nothing to cool the air, it did blow away some of the oppressive humidity. The path they took twisted down and around, and was well lighted until after they'd crossed a section of the highway that ribboned the park. Farther in, streetlights were broken; those still whole were covered by surrounding branches, quite dim.

"Isn't it dangerous in here at night?" Jonathan asked. "Where are we going?"

They passed rows of benches and entered a small clearing which led to the wider expanse of the Sheep Meadow. Dan stopped and lay down on the grass. It was dry, it crackled beneath him.

Reluctantly, Jonathan joined him on the grass, although he remained sitting up. Why had Dan brought them here? It wasn't as eerie as on the path. He could make out large dogs romping in the meadow in the distance, the frail shadows of their masters, leashes in hand, even farther away.

Jonathan lighted a cigarette and kept quiet. For the first time since he'd come into the city today, he felt the quiet around them.

"I used to come here at night, years ago," Dan said. "I used to meet Ian, my first lover, here. I was still married to Janet, and I was afraid she'd find out. So we met here. Came here every night until it got too cold. We first met at the Central Park Zoo men's room. Romantic, huh?"

"Are you sorry now you didn't stay with Ian?" Jonathan asked. Why else would Dan have brought up the subject?

"No. I wouldn't have left Janet for Ian. I didn't, and I saw him almost a year. Whereas with you, well, that was only a few weeks, and I knew I'd have to get a divorce."

"If you're trying to pull a guilt trip on me, forget it."

Dan remained silent: reorganizing his attack?

"If it *was* a misunderstanding with your teenager," Dan began, "what do you plan to do? I don't mean in the next week, or even in the next month. After that. Or have you thought about that?"

"Of course I've thought about it." But Jonathan hadn't, or at least hadn't enough. Everything happened so fast, it surprised him. And it had continued so smoothly up to today, he'd simply assumed it would go on as smoothly, as though proving that it was the natural step for him, for them.

"Well?" Dan prodded. "Aren't you going to tell me?"

"Why should I?"

"Because I'm the one being dropped. And so I have to know *why* after all these years I'm being dropped."

That was why Dan had brought him here, not to moon over memories of the lover who'd gotten away.

"You're not being dropped."

"What do you call it? Or don't you even dignify it with a name?"

Silence again. Of course, now Jonathan was completely guilt-ridden. He *was* dropping Dan. Everyone else would see it that way. Even Janet would be on Dan's side. Yet, yet, there was another way to see it. So he began to explain his position, explaining how Stevie was only symptomatic of a larger change he was going through, of a real change in his life. He found himself repeating his earlier words to Dan on the phone.

"Bullshit!" Dan interrupted. "That's all rationalization. What happened is that you had a brief, exotic affair, with this attractive teenager, and now it's over. That's all. Why try to make something more out of it? At least she had the sense to see what it was—a little affair. How come you can't?"

"You sound completely certain of that," Jonathan said when Dan was done.

"I am."

"Then how do you explain this—even if she won't see me again, you'd better go back to London, now."

Dan sat up. "You mean she was just an excuse."

"She *wasn't* an excuse."

"An excuse for your wanting to break up."

"She wasn't an excuse," Jonathan repeated. Then, and he felt it now, "But yes, I think we ought to break up now. Even if she won't see me again."

"But why?"

"I don't know. I guess I'm just fed up with my life. I want to change it. I suppose I don't like it," Jonathan began. He went on to talk about Balzac's tonight, how the restaurant had symbolized for him everything that seemed wrong about their lives together. How inbred it all was. How expected. How petty.

"That's not so. We have all sorts of friends. Just because we go to a gay restaurant once doesn't mean we're stuck in a ghetto."

Jonathan argued that they were. He felt closed in on all sides, not only here, but at Sea Mist too. His life seemed claustrophobic, his relationships empty and meaningless.

The more he spoke, the more Jonathan himself understood why this crisis had come. It was true. He'd never really thought it through before, but now that he had, it was clear, obvious, and truly a cause for despair. It was sad; he and Dan had good times together. But it was over. Like all good things. And maybe something would happen with Stevie. And maybe—and more likely—nothing. But at least Jonathan didn't have to feel like a play-actor in a dead relationship, automatically going about being someone he wasn't. Even in the relatively dim lighting, Jonathan could see Dan's face harden as he spoke, his eyes flash.

"Are you through?" Dan interrupted. "Because I'd like to say something. I don't know what's gotten to you, whether it's work on your score, or something with your collaborators, or what, but you say you feel a great lack in your life, a great emptiness and meaninglessness. Well, I'm surprised and sorry to hear it, because you never gave me previous evidence of any great lack. No," he warned Jonathan not to interrupt, "I don't feel empty or meaningless. I didn't feel that way when I was twisted around last year with that boy. When I first met you, Jonathan, I said to myself, here he is. This is the brother, the lover, the friend, the boy, the grandfather, the man I've been looking for all my life. That's how I thought you considered me too. I assumed we were together for the duration, thick and thin. It's only since we've been together that I've gained enough confidence to do what I always thought I could never do: to have a career. I had my family, my friends, my career, and I had you. That was enough for me, Jonathan."

Jonathan's guilt washed over him, anger too. All he could say was, "I'm sorry about that, Dan. You were wrong."

"I guess I was. Not only for myself. I don't really understand your complaint anyway. You've got it easy. *We've* got it easy. Look around for a second, will you. Compare yourself, your life, to some of these poor schnooks who work in offices, who can't create, who can't entertain, can't move people, who'll live their lives without being the dozens of characters you and I can imagine. What about those sad queens you see dragging themselves from their desks to bars and nowhere else, people who've never been loved. People envy you. People admire you. People throw themselves at you, if you'd only come down to earth for a minute or two to see them."

"Who?"

"Plenty of people. Amadea. When she looks at you, her face goes blank like someone slapped her."

"Amadea? Are you *sure*?"

"Plenty of people. Guys cruise you left and right. People send over drinks in restaurants as though you *were* a porno star!"

"You arranged that."

"Why bother? Someone else will do it. Nor did I have to arrange your teenager either. Those things happen. You have so much in your life, Jonathan, why are you greedy for more?"

"You don't understand. I'm not greedy for more."

"You are," Dan said, then, "Call it whatever you want." He stood up, brushed off his pants. "If you really feel empty and want to do something meaningful, do it. Join the Peace Corps. Become a social worker. Become a saint. But don't tell me your life is empty, because that implies mine is too. And I don't believe that for a minute."

His anger exploded, Dan calmly added, "I'm going home. And I'll do what you want. I'll call for reservations on the flight to London tomorrow. Crazy as those people sometimes are, at least they aren't beyond hope like you."

He strode ahead, and Jonathan got up and followed him home.

Back in the apartment, Dan immediately dialed for reservations, then announced he was going to bed.

Jonathan unpacked his bags, took out his score and notebooks, and brought them into the second bedroom, which had been set up as his work studio, the walls insulated against the sound of the piano. He sat down, and opened the score, but couldn't concentrate. He tried distracting himself with some other plans for songs he'd previously written. That didn't work either. Even turning on the radio to a classical music station didn't help calm him.

An hour later, Jonathan, too, went to bed. As he supposed, Dan—exhausted by travel, by the day's activities—was already asleep.

Lying next to him in the double bed was like being next to a time bomb ticking. Jonathan couldn't sleep, nor could he quite remain fully awake. He twisted around in the sheets, dozed, awakened for a half hour, then dozed again for another twenty minutes by the face of the reproachful digital clock. Awake again, he tried to read, tried to avoid looking at Dan. That was difficult. How large, how present Dan seemed flat out next to him, compared to Stevie. Dan's tan was almost faded. His face, in profile against the pillow, looked handsomely like that on a cameo or medallion.

Oh, Dan, he thought, look at you! Tomorrow morning you'll wake up with sheet wrinkles all over your face and you'll call out from the bathroom where you're inspecting yourself in the mirror, "I can't go out of the apartment looking like this! People will think we've taken up sadomasochism!"

Tired as Dan was, he was still a most active sleeper. Where did he get his energy from? Awake all last night, then jetting here in the morning, running around the city, getting to Penn Station, then coming back, having dinner, going into the park, arguing. And still not stopped yet, still moving around.

Dan's body always stayed warmer than Jonathan's when he slept—another sign of his intense vitality. Feverish, Dan was like a big bedwarming pan. During his last bout with the flu, every time Jonathan had brushed up against him by accident, he'd felt seared by the touch.

Now Dan was on his back again, shifting position twice in his sleep as Jonathan watched. Dan's head was tilted back, half on, half off the pillow, the sheet covering him had inched down past his midsection. Long, low snores emptied out of him. Even sleeping seemed to be exercise for Dan.

Gray hairs on his chest: the first Jonathan noticed. One or two among Dan's pubic hairs. The large, fleshy volume of his thighs and arms, of his calves and torso. Only an inch taller than Jonathan, Dan was slender-looking because his weight was distributed well.

When they'd last weighed themselves together, Dan had been more than twenty pounds heavier. Big bones. Lots of muscle and flesh. He was essentially a country boy, from the north fork of Long Island, with his bright chestnut hair and WASP-y facial features. Dan's hair had glowed red under the sunny sky that first time Jonathan had seen him at the Bethesda Fountain in the park. Since then it had glimmered orange on beaches and under strobe lights, been dyed to auburn on misty afternoons, had become a bronzed helmet during drugged hallucinations.

Ladies and gentleman, my lover! Or rather, my ex-lover. No, that wasn't exactly right, was it? You couldn't take back love once given, could you? So that someone once intensely loved was no longer perceived as having been loved. No, impossible. Love didn't flash on and off like a light, like lightwaves, only striking one person, one object, and nothing else. Or rather, yes, love did seem to be like that, on the surface; but it acted differently too. As though it were a material, given and received, forever attached to the receiver. You could suddenly hate someone once loved, but that didn't subtract from having loved before. It meant, instead, the addition of another, opposite energy. Love was both a wave *and* a material, then. A wavelike material. Didn't that define something else too?...Of course it did. Sophisticated experiments on the most minute atomic particles had shown them to be both waves and matter at different times. That meant that love was like atomic structures, the very stuff of the universe.

Then Fiammetta wasn't merely an idealist. She'd given the memory of her falcon a materiality far exceeding what it had really possessed. And if no bird could compare, it was because Fiammetta already possessed it fully. As Gentile, her suitor, possessed her fully too, loving her.

As Jonathan possessed Dan, Barry Meade, Amadea and Saul, Artie and Ken and Janet, all his other friends, all the people who adored his music, those who sang it on stage, in cabarets, in shower stalls, those who recorded it, who hummed along with it, who sent him drinks anonymously. Why then, possessing so much, had he needed Stevie too? Losing her, why did he no longer want his fans, his friends, his collaborators, Dan, anymore?

It was impossible to figure out. He should get some sleep.

But he couldn't. As soon as the bed light was shut off again, Dan became restless in his sleep. At first, he mumbled. Then he began speaking disjointedly, short half words blustering out of him, then broken whispers.

He was having one of his big dreams, a Cecil B. DeMille, as Dan called them. He was dreaming that he was on location, or on-stage, or on a sound set, or in a story conference room. He was reliving, or replaying, or preparing for some work-related encounter: talking to a film actress, trying to persuade a producer or scriptwriter that something had to be changed. He would be animated, suddenly laugh, then be quiet again. He even performed in his sleep, damn him!

Jonathan sat up and lighted his bed lamp. He'd never get to sleep without a pill with Dan carrying on like this. Jonathan didn't want to wake up tomorrow with a drug hangover; he didn't want to feel foggy and vague until his second large mug of coffee. Or did he? It might prove a good way to not deal with Dan.

When he returned to the bedroom with a glass of water to wash the sleeping pill down, he saw that Dan had assumed a peculiar position. His knees were drawn up toward his chest, his arms across his face. The sheets were pushed completely off. He was very agitated, still talking in his sleep, but oddly, gutturally, the words difficult to make out. His lips moved, his head thrashed on the pillow from side to side.

Jonathan had seen Dan happy, passionate, even angry in his sleep, but he'd never seen him frightened. Dan seemed very fearful now. He flinched, as though struck. He pulled away, as though avoiding being punched in the chest or face. Fascinated, Jonathan put the glass of water on the side table and kneeled on the mattress watching him more closely.

Dan flinched again, his arms protecting his face, as though warding off blows. He whimpered, then drew back to receive another invisible blow, his face contorted with anger and terror. The attack seemed to worsen, the bed began to shake with Dan's contortions. It seemed as though Dan were being beaten up as he slept. Jonathan had never witnessed anything like it before.

Watching, Jonathan went from fascination, to feeling satisfaction, even to feeling vengeful; but that soon altered to helplessness in the face of some terrible, invisible thing that swooped past him to strike at Dan as he slept. As the bizarre attack seemed to become more intense, Jonathan began to feel afraid himself, as though a battle were being fought in which he counted but in which he was unable to contend. He'd awakened Dan from dreams before, sometimes he'd suffered from them. But this was different, so chilling that it made the hair stand up on the back of his neck, as though some ghost, some horror was counting on his very indifference. Watching Dan, Jonathan was suddenly ravaged to the heart.

As suddenly, he realized he faced a choice. He could wake Dan up from his nightmare, or he could get out of bed, close the bedroom door, take the pill, and sleep undisturbed on the sofa in his studio. Both choices were insignificant actions. But each held far-reaching consequences, each would determine the rest of his life. If he left Dan now that meant he was leaving him forever—it meant it in a way his earlier words to Dan hadn't meant it, meant it even though Dan would probably never know how it happened, here as he slept and had a nightmare. Was that what Jonathan wanted?

He got off the bed, looking away from Dan. He could still hear his movements, his stifled cries of fear. But he couldn't face him. Not for a minute or so. He had to think.

Outside the bedroom window, Central Park stretched in a darkness made only dimmer by the punctuation of tiny streetlights within its black masses of trees. Across the park, on the East Side, building lights were few; the skyline formed a continuous ebony silhouette against the humid gray sky. It was three fifteen. Hadn't Scott Fitzgerald written of the desolation of three o'clock in the morning? Hadn't Gerard Manley Hopkins written of the torture of sudden emptiness at such an hour, "Not, I'll not, carrion comfort,

Despair, not feast on thee; / Not untwist—slack though they may be—these last strands of man / In me…" What was Jonathan to do?

Words. Hollow words. Where was the music, the halting, tragic, unending dirge that ought to accompany them? What was he to do?

If he left now, he left forever, gave himself forever to solitude, to despair. There might be Stevie, other Stevies, other Steves, even. Never another Daniel. But if he awakened Dan, it would begin all over again, continue, this shadow of a life he'd only just recognized tonight, this unendurable life. What was he to do?

Behind him, Dan whimpered on. Help Dan? Help himself?

"Help me decide," he cried inwardly, though to whom he didn't know. "Help me. Please help me!"

He was suddenly aware of quiet behind him. He turned, realized his hands were clenched over his face, let them down, and saw Dan, awake, half up on his elbows, staring at him. Dan's face glittered with perspiration, his long hair was matted with sweat. He breathed deeply, irregularly. He looked at Jonathan with a glazed expression, as though still half dreaming.

"You were having a nightmare," Jonathan said. He could barely get the words out; they broke on his tongue, spilled out, dribbling out of his lips.

Dan seemed to awaken fully. He still stared at Jonathan, who felt the need to explain.

"I didn't know whether to go or to stay and wake you. For the first time in my life, Dan, I didn't know what to do!"

He kneeled on the bed.

"I had no idea, Dan. None!"

"Shh," Dan said, and Jonathan realized he had been shouting. He must have shouted before, calling for help. Had his calls before been vocalized? Had they awakened Dan?

"You were having this nightmare, see," Jonathan repeated, "You were being attacked or something."

"It's over. Don't worry about it," Dan said, his voice calm.

"It was horrible, Dan. I couldn't stand watching you like that. But I didn't know what to do."

Daniel held out his arms. Jonathan looked at them blankly.

"It was horrible," Jonathan repeated in a hoarse whisper. "I was so frightened."

Dan leaned forward, put his arms around Jonathan, and drew him to his breast. Jonathan could feel the heat from Dan's arms around him, Dan's sweat-beaded skin cooling, slightly clammy. His own body trembled. Their hearts thudded.

For an instant, he pictured himself like that butterfly on the beach at Sea Mist, its beautifully colored wings held tight in the grip of a dead sandcrab. The image revolted him. He shuddered at it, tried to get it out of his mind, and almost pulled away from Dan.

Dan hushed him again, held him close again.

After a long time, Dan said, "That dream was a grade-B horror show. Written by Poe, directed by Hitchcock. Maybe when I'm done with the BBC I should look for a thriller project." He went on in that vein for another minute, throwing out ideas, books that had never been made into films that might fill the bill; he almost decided on one. "Incidentally," Dan concluded, "thanks for waking me up."

Jonathan wanted to say that he hadn't, that what really happened was… He didn't say it. Dan didn't seem to want to hear it, anyway. Their bodies fit together, as they always had, and their hearts had slowed down to normal and beat with a strong, regular, identical beat. Nothing else mattered. In his worst moment of despair, without being aware of it, Jonathan had made his choice; his despair had made the choice for him. He let himself be held.

AFTERWORD

Only recently, a friend reminded me of what I said upon the publication of *Late in the Season* in 1981, "It was sort of a bargain book for me: You know, write four novels, get one free?"

I was trying to explain how quickly and easily this novel arrived, fully formed as it were, and how quickly and easily it was written: a mere twenty-five days for the first handwritten draft, another five weeks for a revised typed draft. Compare this to a year or more of work for all of my other novels.

According to the little ledger, wherein I've listed my works and their publication since 1971, *Late in the Season* was immediately preceded by the second of my *Window Elegies* poems and by three short stories, "Teddy the Hook," "Spinning," and "A Stroke," all of which were quickly published, the first two in *Blueboy* magazine, the third in a literary quarterly no longer extant. The stories later appeared in my popular 1983 collection, *Slashed to Ribbons in Defense of Love.* For the next year, following the completion of the novel, I wrote only poems, essays, and book reviews. Obviously, the novel satisfied me for a while.

That *Late in the Season* came so easily is due to three factors. First, I knew the book's Fire Island Pines background and so didn't have to research it, as I'd had to for the previous two, much longer, more detailed books, *The Mesmerist* and *The Lure.* I'd lived at the Pines as a summer resident for the past five years and knew the place as well as anyone in terms of its flora, fauna, and seasonal change. Given how small it was, even if you included nearby Cherry

Grove and Water Island, geographically and, in terms of population, it was nothing more really than a small town: easily comprehended and equally easy to render.

It was this ambience of an American small town with a twist that I was trying to convey in the book. As well as the idea of a "summer place," a partly stable, partly transient community intrinsically different from other resorts around the world.

A second factor was that I felt strongly impelled by the very autobiographical story of the novel; impelled to write it out in the hope that I might somehow understand why the romance had gone so totally awry, despite all of my conscious efforts.

The end of that relationship caused me great anguish. And, coming as it had at exactly the same time as the extraordinary popular and critical (one might say "cultural") success of my novel *The Lure*, had caused a strange psychic rift to open in me: a conflict between what I believed life was capable of bringing me and what I was experiencing. I sensed some screwy equation between artistic success and failed love that I kept praying was not or would not become a life pattern. I remember one afternoon when, within a five-minute span, I received incredibly good career news and the worst possible news about my love affair. I desperately needed to heal that inner rift before it turned into severe depression, schizophrenia, whatever. As I'd done for over a decade, I once more turned to writing as a tool for self-healing, for self-redefinition.

A few words about this romance. Like the one in the novel, it was a triangle, and, like the young woman in the novel, I was the third party intruding into a gay marriage. Yes, I was Stevie—not Jonathan. Unlike Stevie, I wasn't aware a marriage existed until I was in very deep. But like her, once I was aware of it, I came to believe it was not a strong relationship and would not survive work on my part to end it. Like Stevie, once I'd made that clear to the young man I loved and he expressed a wish to continue the marriage anyway, I sacrificed myself and split, hating myself for taking the high road. Unlike Jonathan and Daniel's marriage, the real one didn't last once I was gone.

A third factor for the book being relatively fast and easy to write was that I'd grown tired of the post-Flaubert, tightly written, point-of-view novel, which, in their own way, my first four novels all had been. Now I wanted to experiment.

Late in the Season turned out to break the mold less than I'd hoped. Instead, like the next two non-gay-themed novels, *House of Cards* and *To the Seventh Power*, it was a further exploration of how to tell a story from multiple points of view. Evidently I hadn't worked all of that area quite yet.

On the other hand, this novel was experimental for me another way: It successfully got me past the concept of the "perfect" novel. Instead of writing a book that had to be laid out like a diagram, each hour and place and action and emotion graphed to within an inch of its life, *Late in the Season* was written almost impromptu, as though I were doing prose-poems. Feeling, mood, and atmosphere dominated action and plot. If one can (invidiously) compare writing to painting, *The Lure* was a large mural (or series of murals) while *Late in the Season* was a watercolor (or series of aquarelles). Where my other novels depended upon fully modeled characters and totally detailed settings, this was more a sketchbook, where the "white" space—what was not narrated, or said—was as crucial as what was.

I would have to construct a new form, a hybrid of fiction and the memoir, or as one publisher put it, "a memoir in the form of a novel," to fully break away from those stylistic precursors who'd influenced me. Especially the great Henry James, who has been the cause of much of the best and worst writing of our time. Because as it turned out, how to restructure wasn't the problem I had to solve to go on and develop as a writer, but rather how to retexture. By the time I came to write *Ambidextrous,* it was clear I had to not only stress my own voice and style, I also had to design a new way to narrate that would be no one's but mine, one capable of the color, scenic power, emotional depth, drama, philosophizing, and character drawing of the masters.

The following volumes, *Men Who Loved Me* and *A House on the Ocean, a House on the Bay* (also about Fire Island) continued to develop this new texturing. Even my novel *Like People in History* uses it, while pretending to be first-person point of view—a slyness that has elicited the most hilariously irrelevant, boneheaded reviews a book of mine has ever received.

In that sense, *Late in the Season* is a transitional work, on the way from one fully formed style—even period—to another. Because of that, because of how easy it was to write, and because of its ability even today to revivify for me the emotional situation and period of time in which it was written, it will probably always remain a favorite.

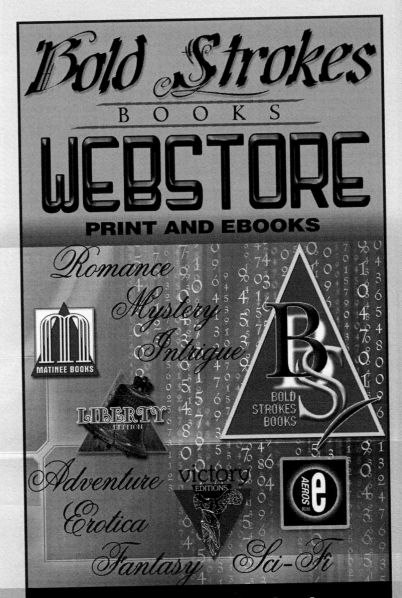